FROM THE
NANCY DREW FILES

THE CASE: *Someone has been doctoring Spotless, a new skin cream, with a deadly poison.*

CONTACT: *Ned's college marketing class is competing for a plush ad agency job by giving out free samples of Spotless.*

SUSPECTS: *Marcia Grafton—ambition and jealousy are a dangerous combination.*

Justin Dodd—he used to work for the competition. Is he still loyal to his old employer?

Heather Tompkins—her interest in Ned may be more than friendship.

COMPLICATIONS: *Nancy seems to have a romantic rival, and Bess has a crush on one of the leading suspects.*

Books in The Nancy Drew™ Series

THE NANCY DREW FILES CASE · 41

SOMETHING TO HIDE

Carolyn Keene

AN ARCHWAY PAPERBACK
Published by SIMON & SCHUSTER
New York   London   Toronto   Sydney   Tokyo   Singapore

An Archway paperback
first published in Great Britain
by Simon & Schuster Ltd in 1992
A Paramount Communications Company

Copyright © 1988 by Simon & Schuster Inc.

Simon & Schuster Ltd
West Garden Place
Kendal Street
London W2 2AQ

NANCY DREW, AN ARCHWAY PAPERBACK
and colophon are registered trademarks of Simon & Schuster Inc.

THE NANCY DREW FILES is a trademark
of Simon & Schuster Inc.

Simon & Schuster of Australia Pty Ltd
Sydney

A CIP catalogue record for this book is
available from the British Library

ISBN 0-671-71657-3

Printed and bound in Great Britain by
HarperCollins Manufacturing, Glasgow

SOMETHING TO HIDE

Chapter

One

"THIS SHOULD BE FUN," George Fayne said. As George rang the doorbell to her cousin Bess Marvin's house, a soft October breeze ruffled her short dark hair.

"What I think is so great," Nancy Drew said, pushing her reddish blond hair back from her face, "is all the time I'm going to get to spend with Ned!"

Nancy's boyfriend, Ned Nickerson, had come home from Emerson College for a long weekend to work on a research project for a marketing class he was taking, and Nancy and her friends were going to help him. It wasn't

1

often that Nancy and Ned had time together during the school year, and Nancy couldn't wait.

George shot Nancy a teasing glance. "Well, I don't know about you, Drew, but I'm thinking of this as an *educational* experience."

The door opened just then, and Bess Marvin stood on the doorstep, a tissue in her hand. "I'm ready if you are," she croaked.

"Bess, you look terrible!" Nancy exclaimed. Although Bess had done her best to cover her red nose with makeup, the flame color still showed through. Her blue eyes were watery and running. "Are you sure you feel up to this?"

Bess blew her nose and cleared her throat vigorously before tossing back her long blond hair. "Just try to keep me away," she challenged.

"She has a point," George put in. "Bess can always get herself together to go to the mall."

Bess made a face at her cousin before slipping on a pair of sunglasses to hide her red eyes. "You'll never understand about shopping. You spend all your time in sweats and running shoes." She turned to Nancy. "Honestly, Nan, I'll be fine. I sound a lot worse than I feel. Come on, let's go!"

"What exactly are we going to do for this research project?" George asked once the three friends were in Nancy's Mustang and on their way to the mall.

"Ned didn't tell me too much," Nancy said. "Only that a group of students from his marketing class would be working at the River Heights Mall introducing people to a new product."

"What's the product?" said George.

"He didn't tell me that, either." Nancy smiled. "Actually, he was very mysterious about the whole thing."

Bess hardly listened to any more of their conversation. Instead, she leaned forward from the back seat to study herself in the rearview mirror. "I just wish I didn't look so horrible today," she fretted.

"What are you talking about?" George asked.

Bess pointed to a small blemish on her left cheek. "I never break out! Why now, when I'm about to be spending a whole Saturday with cute college boys? It's not fair!" Bess grimaced.

"Oh, you look fine," George reassured her as they pulled into the mall's parking lot.

"All I can say is nothing seems to be going right for me today," Bess croaked, clambering out of the back seat.

Glancing at the entrance to the mall, Nancy felt a smile pass over her face. Pacing back and forth in front of the mall, waiting for them, was Ned. She recognized him instantly by his tall build.

Nancy walked on ahead of her friends, stole up behind Ned, and threw her arms around him. "Oh, Ned!" she murmured in his ear. "It's so good to see you!"

"Nancy!" Ned turned and gave her a big hug, smiling down into her eyes. "I really missed you!" He reached out and gently drew Nancy's face up to his, then softly kissed her lips. Nancy felt a warm glow pass through her.

"Ahem, you two. When do we get to meet the rest of the research team?" George asked.

Ned grinned. "Follow me." He put his arm around Nancy and led the girls inside the mall and over to a sleek little booth with mirrored sides and a pink awning. "Welcome to the Spotless project!" he said grandly. "And here are two members of the team that's going to make Emerson College history," he went on.

"We hope," said a tall, angular girl behind the counter. She had long golden hair and pale skin and was dressed all in black. She gave Nancy and her friends a polite half-smile. "I'm Marcia Grafton," she said.

"And I'm Justin Dodd, the brains behind this operation!" boomed her companion.

Marcia winced. "He's got his name right, anyway," she said.

Justin was short and chubby, with curly

4

brown hair and a snub nose. He gave the three girls a friendly grin. "Nice to have you aboard," he said. "Welcome to the ultra-glamorous world of market research." He laughed loudly.

Nancy smiled back at him. "Nice to be here," she said.

"Don't pay any attention to Justin's little ways," Marcia said tiredly. "He's the class clown—if you haven't already figured that out. I'm glad you can give us a hand."

"What did you want us to do?" George asked.

Marcia picked up one of the little white jars from the table in the middle of the booth. "We're giving away free samples of this," she said. "Some of us will hand them out while the rest of us get people to fill out questionnaires."

"What's in the jars?" Bess asked hoarsely.

"It's a preventive cream," Marcia answered. "You put it on every night, and it keeps your skin from breaking out. It really works, too."

"It's called Spotless. Spotless! Get it?" Justin asked, nudging Nancy.

"We're using River Heights as a test area," Ned explained.

"And if it's successful here?" asked George.

"Then the company will start a national sales campaign. Here comes the rest of our team." Ned walked over to greet a couple who had come up to the booth. "Meet Heather Tompkins and Brad Chanin. Heather and Brad, this is Nancy Drew, Bess Marvin, and George Fayne."

Heather shook her mane of brown curls back from her perfect heart-shaped face. Her long-lashed hazel eyes darted from Nancy to Bess and George. "Hello," she said, shaking Nancy's hand.

Brad Chanin was blond and tall, with shoulders a football player would have envied. Behind his horn-rimmed glasses his deep blue eyes were sparkling.

"It's nice to meet you," he said to the three girls, but he directed his gaze only at Bess.

"Ready to start?" asked Ned.

"We sure are," Brad said enthusiastically.

The group moved into position at the booth. As the mall began to fill with shoppers, Ned and Justin approached teenagers, while— under Marcia's direction—Nancy, George, and Heather asked them to fill out questionnaires. Bess and Brad sat at the table, arranging the sample jars and filing the questionnaires as they were turned in.

"This really won't take long," Nancy promised a redheaded girl who was glancing worriedly at her watch. "All we need to know are your name, address, age, and what creams you've used in the past."

"Well, I guess it's worth it if Spotless

works," answered the girl. "I've tried just about everything."

"It works," Heather assured her. "Believe me, it works!"

"How did you all get involved in this test?" Nancy asked Heather as the redheaded girl turned in her questionnaire and walked away.

"Didn't Ned tell you?" Heather asked. Nancy shook her head and Heather went on. "We're all senior marketing majors at Emerson—except for Ned, but he was taking a course with us, so he was asked to help."

"I hate to sound dumb," George said as she leaned against the back of the booth, "but what exactly *is* marketing?"

Marcia tucked her long blond hair behind one ear. "Basically, it's anything that convinces people to buy a product," she said.

"And giveaways like this are part of it," Heather added. "Our professor calls it market research. I call it testing the waters before you jump in."

"Yeah," Justin said, turning around. "After all, who wants to drown in a pool of skin cream?" He doubled up in laughter as Heather rolled her eyes.

"Well, it certainly seems like a great project," said George.

"It's more than that," Marcia said sharply. "There's a lot at stake!"

Nancy stared at her in surprise. Before Nancy could ask Marcia what she meant, another group of teenagers arrived, and the girls were busy once again.

Half an hour later, when the crowd had thinned out a little, Nancy moved to Ned's side. "How's it going?" she asked, pulling him a few feet away from the booth.

"Great!" Ned smiled at Nancy. "And I think being in River Heights has something to do with it."

Nancy returned the smile, their thoughts on the same wavelength.

"Is this a private conversation, or can anyone join?" Heather had left the table and moved up beside Ned. "I'd certainly hate to be left out," she cooed, looking at Ned in a way that definitely excluded Nancy.

Nancy found herself wondering what was going on with Heather. Didn't the girl know Ned was her boyfriend? Why was she flirting with him?

"I just think this is a fabulous project," Heather said, her eyes never leaving Ned. "We're really lucky to be part of it."

Ned nodded and squeezed Nancy's hand. Obviously he wasn't responding to Heather.

Nancy turned back to the sample table. Justin was joking with a group of customers while George was helping a boy with his questionnaire. There was another boy waiting to fill in a questionnaire, but Marcia hadn't noticed him. Her eyes were fixed on the sample table, where Bess and Brad were sitting. There was a frown on her face.

Bess was talking animatedly to Brad. He was leaning over her, his blond head bent as though he was afraid of missing a single word.

Nancy glanced back at Marcia. The thin girl's fists were clenched. Something about Bess and Brad was definitely bugging her.

Nancy decided she'd better intervene. She walked nonchalantly over to the table. "How's your throat, Bess?" she asked.

"No worse," Bess said cheerfully. "In fact, it's feeling a little better."

"Your turn to do questionnaires, then," said Nancy. As Bess rose from behind the table, Nancy slipped into the seat her friend had just left.

Nancy turned to Brad. "Do you live around here?" she asked him.

"Right outside River Heights, in Clinton," said Brad. "So does Heather. Marcia's from River Heights now. Her folks just moved here." Justin, Nancy knew, was from River Heights itself. He had gone to a private school and graduated two years before Ned. "My folks are glad I'm home," Brad continued. "It's—"

"Hey, Chanin!" came Justin's loud voice. "I'm going out to the car to get more samples. Don't let anyone steal anything while I'm

9

gone!" He grinned and bounced off toward the exit.

Heather had strolled back to the booth and let out an exasperated sigh. "There goes the mad scientist," she said.

"Why do you call him that?" asked George. "He doesn't look anything like one to me."

"All that kidding around is an act," Heather answered. "Justin's pretty intense. You should see him at finals time—no joking around then."

"So you're all in classes together?" George asked.

"Sure. There aren't that many marketing majors at Emerson," Brad explained as Marcia walked over to join their conversation.

"It's true. We're kind of like brothers and sisters," added Heather. "Right, Marcia?"

Marcia didn't answer. She just stared at Heather. Unruffled, Heather gazed calmly back at her.

There's something going on that I don't understand, Nancy said to herself. Marcia's definitely upset—but about what specifically? It's got to be something to do with Brad. I wonder if—

"Did you all miss me?"

Justin interrupted Nancy's train of thought. He walked up with a new box of Spotless samples and dumped them on the table. "You know, I'd forgotten it was almost Halloween until I saw the store windows," he commented. "Since we're all going to be in River Heights for the next few days, why don't we have a party?"

"Sounds good!" said Heather. It wasn't Nancy's imagination that Heather glanced over at Ned that time.

"We can have it at my house Tuesday night," Justin added. "Want to make it a costume party?"

"A party with just the five of us?" Marcia asked a little snidely.

"Well, I'm sure Bess would like to come," Brad said gallantly. "And Nancy and George, of course," he added. "And we all have some other friends who still live around here."

"Looks like we've got ourselves a party," said Justin. "But what are we going to do for fun tonight? And don't suggest that we fill out any more questionnaires."

Heather laughed. "I won't. Everyone's welcome at my house tonight. We can send out for pizza." She glanced sideways at Ned. "Lucky my parents are out of town." There was no mistaking her motive that time, Nancy decided.

"You three will come, won't you?" Brad asked Nancy, George, and Bess. But once again he seemed to be talking only to Bess.

"We'd love to," Bess answered him. With a laugh, she added, "I guess I'll start making myself beautiful right now. Let's see if this stuff really works!"

She reached for one of the sample jars of Spotless, opened the lid, and dabbed a little of the cream on her cheek.

Without any warning, Justin lunged for Bess. He knocked the jar out of her hand with a swift blow.

"Stop!" he shouted. "Don't do it! That stuff is dangerous!"

Chapter

Two

"WHAT DO YOU MEAN—dangerous?" Bess cried. She grabbed a tissue and frantically began scrubbing her cheek.

"What's in that cream?" Nancy demanded sharply. "Why are we giving away free samples if there's something the matter with it?"

Justin flushed and sheepishly ran his hand through his curly hair. "I—I— Aw, come on, guys. Can't you take a joke? I was only fooling!"

"That's not my idea of a joke," George snapped. Bess just stared at him.

Nancy echoed George's anger. "You seemed

pretty convincing just now, Justin. Why did you pull a stunt like that?" she asked.

"I'm always kidding around!" Justin protested. He laughed feebly and shrugged.

Brad came up behind Bess and put a comforting hand on her shoulder. Then he turned his attention to Justin. "I get the feeling you're holding something back. Like something you may have learned last summer?"

Justin's smile vanished instantly. For a moment he didn't answer. Then he lowered his gaze to the floor, as if he couldn't meet Brad's accusing eyes.

"So I worked for Asco last summer," he muttered finally. "There's no crime in that."

"Wait a minute," Nancy broke in. "Isn't Asco that pharmaceuticals company on LeBlond Avenue?"

"That's right. And they're the biggest potential competitor to Spotless," Marcia answered. "Their skin cream is called Clearly. But maybe you should get Justin to tell you about them."

"Asco is incredibly ruthless," Brad added darkly. "They'd do anything to make Clearly number one. Anything."

"Hold on!" Justin protested. His chubby face was utterly serious now. "They may be rival companies, but Asco wouldn't do something underhanded. They don't need to. Clearly's a good product."

"What does Asco know about Spotless?"

asked Brad accusingly. "You haven't told them anything, have you?"

"Of course I haven't!" sputtered Justin. "Honestly, I was only kidding Bess. I just wanted to liven things up, you know?"

"Well, you sure picked a strange way," Heather said. Everyone nodded in agreement.

At that moment a fresh wave of teenagers approached the booth. For the next few minutes, no one had time for anything but handing out samples and questionnaires.

The second there was a lull, Nancy asked Justin another question. "What exactly did you do at Asco?" she said.

Everyone at the booth paused to listen to Justin's answer.

Nervously he ran his hand through his hair. "I worked in their labs as a summer intern," he answered. "I was a chemistry major last year, so I guess they thought I was a good fit."

"But now you're majoring in marketing?" George asked. "That's kind of an unusual change of majors, isn't it?"

Justin opened his mouth, then closed it again. "I found out that I wasn't a very good chemist," he said finally. "But I had taken a couple of marketing courses and had a flair for it. So now I'm in the marketing program. Okay? Are you all satisfied?"

There was an edge in Justin's voice now. "If the question-and-answer period is over now,

I'd like to get some more samples from the car." With that, he strode away from the booth.

Heather pointed at the sample table. "Didn't he notice that we've got plenty?" she asked. The table was still covered with jars.

"Maybe he just couldn't face us anymore," said Marcia. She slid a pile of completed questionnaires into a large envelope. "Don't you think we ought to tell the ad agency about him?"

To Nancy's surprise, Heather burst into laughter. "Marcia, you just want him to drop out of the program. That way you'd have less competition. Come on, admit I'm right!"

"What competition?" George asked in bewilderment. "I'm lost."

Marcia tossed back her hair and shot Heather a hostile look. "Didn't Ned tell you?" she asked George.

"Tell us what?" Nancy asked.

"There's more than grades at stake in this project," Marcia explained. "There's a great job after graduation for the top student. We're getting rated by Spotless's ad agency—the Premier Advertising Agency, in Chicago—on how well we do. The one who does best gets hired by the agency."

"And Marcia just knows she's going to be that Premier person," Heather said mockingly.

The smile Marcia gave her looked very stiff. "At least I'm going to try hard for it," she shot back. "Unlike some people I could mention."

Nancy, Bess, and George exchanged a look. There seemed to be a lot of tension among the participants in this college project.

Nancy felt a warm hand on her shoulder and turned to see Ned smiling down at her.

"Feel like taking a break?" he asked. "I could use some fresh air."

The booth wasn't crowded, so Nancy nodded, and the two of them headed out of the mall, arm in arm.

Nancy blinked in the sudden sunshine. It was a crisp October day. The sun felt warm on Nancy's head and shoulders.

"Well," said Ned ruefully, "I guess you learned how boring market research can be." He took Nancy's hand in his and laced his fingers through hers.

"Oh, I don't know. I think it's all interesting," Nancy said sincerely. "Besides, I wouldn't care even if it were horrible. I love getting to be with you," she added.

Ned leaned over and brushed a kiss on her cheek. "Having you here makes it special for me, too," he said. He squeezed her hand. "Do you feel like going to a movie tonight?" he asked.

"We can't. Remember?" Nancy said. "Heather's having everyone over for pizza."

"Oh, that's right," said Ned. "Well, tomorrow, then."

"You've got yourself a date, Mr. Nickerson," Nancy told him happily. "I'll bet Brad asks Bess out, too. They seem to have hit it off."

"They sure do," Ned agreed. "I hope it works out. To tell you the truth, Nancy, I've been worried about Brad. There's so much competition in this program that I thought it might be getting to him."

"I got a hint of that from Heather and Marcia," Nancy said. "They tried to make it sound like a joke, but I think they were serious."

"It is serious. The job with that ad agency is terrific for someone just out of college," Ned told her. "Whoever wins will be part of the Premier training program, so they'll get fantastic experience. On top of that, the pay is great."

"But how did Premier happen to pick the marketing majors at Emerson to compete for this job?" Nancy asked.

Ned laughed. "Connections. The president of the agency is an Emerson graduate."

"And how does Premier plan on picking who gets the job?" Nancy asked.

"Well, it's a combination of grades and attitude," said Ned. "And we have to write up reports of what we learned from marketing Spotless. Those will count for a lot. I've heard

rumors, too—I don't know if they're true—
that Premier's got someone checking on all the
groups who are manning these test-marketing
booths. You know—seeing if we're giving
service with a smile. That kind of thing."

"Well, for your group's sake, I hope no one
from Premier was at the mall this morning,"
Nancy said dryly. "I feel sorry for all of you,
Ned. It must be tough competing with your
friends."

"At least I don't want the job," Ned said.
"But you're right, Nan—this kind of competition can put a strain on even the best friend-
ships. That's why it's good to see Brad relaxing
again."

Ned sighed and put his arm around Nancy's
shoulder. "You know, I wish I could steal you
away from here, but I guess we'd better get
back inside."

The Spotless booth was surrounded by teenagers when Nancy and Ned got back inside.
Bess and Brad were working as a team; Bess
gave out questionnaires to each of the people
who took samples from Brad. Marcia was
handing out samples with her back to Brad
and Bess. Nancy wasn't sure if that was deliberate or not.

Justin had come back and was looking like
his jolly self again. "You and I get the next
break," he said to Heather as Nancy and Ned
rejoined the group.

"Not until these crowds thin out." There was a sharp edge to Marcia's voice, and she narrowed her eyes as she looked at Nancy. "We've been swamped while you two were gone."

"Sorry," Nancy said mildly. She picked up a clipboard and turned to the next person waiting for a questionnaire. "Oh, no! Someone's run off with my pencil," she said, looking around. "Does anyone have an extra?"

George was about to hand her one, when Justin pulled out a gold pen. "Here you go," he said.

Pretty fancy pen for a college kid, Nancy mused as she clicked it open and began to write. Justin really was eccentric, she thought. He even used brown ink instead of black or blue.

With George's help, Nancy was busy interviewing the kids standing around the booth, when Bess suddenly doubled over in a coughing fit. Nancy turned to her with concern.

"Are you okay, Bess?" asked Brad. "That's a nasty cough!"

Bess looked pale, and Nancy noticed that she was having trouble breathing. "Sure, I'm fine," she said, but her voice was little more than a hoarse whisper.

"You don't sound fine to me," George said. "Why don't I take you home? I'm sure Nancy will let us use her car."

"No, please. I'll be fine!" Bess insisted. "My throat just hurts a little, that's all."

Brad leaned closer to her. "Let me get you something for it," he said. "What about some cough drops? There's a drugstore at the other end of the mall."

Bess looked up at him gratefully. "I don't need any cough drops, but I would love something to drink," she said.

"Some lemonade?" George suggested. "We could go to the Florida Fresh."

"One large lemonade coming up," Brad said promptly. "Anyone else want something to drink?"

When he'd taken everyone's order, Brad looked searchingly at Bess. "You'll be okay, won't you?"

"It's just a sore throat," Justin said. "You can leave her for three minutes, Chanin."

Brad flushed and turned to walk down to the juice stand. When he was out of earshot, Marcia suddenly stood up. "I think he may need some help with all those drinks," she said, and hurried to catch up with him.

Nancy was about to ask Bess if she was sure she didn't want to go home, when she glanced down the promenade and saw Marcia gesturing furiously at Brad. And Nancy could tell Brad was pretty angry himself.

"I wonder what they're fighting about," Nancy remarked softly to Ned.

Ned was looking serious. "They were going out until about a month ago," he said. "I guess Marcia must be mad that Brad's so interested in Bess. He hasn't exactly been hiding it."

So that was it. Marcia still liked Brad, which explained why she seemed so jumpy and irritable around him.

But when Brad and Marcia returned with the drinks, they were both smiling. "Here you go, Bess," said Brad. "And the rest of you, too."

As Bess took her lemonade from his hand, she almost dropped the cup. "Sorry," she said. "My hand felt funny all of a sudden. Must be from filling out all those questionnaires." She took a sip of lemonade. "This tastes great. My throat feels better already."

But Nancy thought her friend still looked pale. "Why don't you sit down for a little while?" she suggested. "We can handle things."

Bess didn't protest. She sank into a chair with a little sigh and leaned her head against her hand.

There were fewer shoppers in the mall now. It was close to closing time, when they'd all be able to go home.

At five o'clock Justin slammed his clipboard down on the table. "Quittin' time!" he shouted. "I'm out of here!"

"Hold on just a minute," Marcia said tartly. "We still have to pack up all our stuff."

Nancy put down her clipboard and turned around to where Bess was sitting at the back of the booth.

"Almost ready to go, Bess?" she asked. Then Nancy looked more closely at her friend. Bess was slumped over in her chair, breathing heavily. Her eyes were glassy, and there was a feverish spot of color on each cheek.

"I feel funny," Bess said in a weak voice when she saw Nancy's eyes on her.

Nancy was at her side immediately. "What's wrong?" she asked.

Bess's eyes rolled back in her head.

Before Nancy could do anything, Bess had slid out of her chair and toppled to the floor in a dead faint.

Chapter

Three

NANCY FLUNG HERSELF DOWN on her knees next to Bess.

"We've got to get her home right away!" Nancy cried. "Ned—George—help me carry her to the car."

Bess's eyes flickered open. "Wh-what's the matter?" she asked in a dazed voice, struggling to sit up. Her face was still deathly pale.

Nancy put a hand on Bess's shoulder. "You fainted," she told her friend gently. "Don't try to move too fast, Bess."

Now George, too, was bending over Bess. "What happened, Bess?" she asked. "You never faint." George looked as worried as Nancy felt. Both of them knew something was really wrong.

"I don't know what happened," said Bess weakly. "I just started feeling dizzy, and then everything went black." Bess put her hands to her head. "I'm still woozy, and my head—oh, it hurts so much!" Bess sounded almost as though she might cry.

"Well, forget about taking you home. This sounds much more serious than a cold. We're taking you to the hospital right now," Nancy said with determination. "They'll find out what's wrong."

"I'm going with you," Brad said in a worried voice. He turned to his classmates. "Will you guys be okay here?"

Marcia gave him a cold stare, then turned away. "We'll have to be, I guess," she said. "Don't worry about us. We'll just finish packing up the stuff and then go home."

Nancy was shocked at the harsh tone in Marcia's voice. She didn't seem to care about Bess and her fainting spell. She sounded as if Bess's collapse was just the topper to a trying day. Of course, Marcia did hardly know Bess, Nancy reminded herself. Still . . .

"Let me give you my address, in case you can come over to my house later," Heather added. Her eyes gave the merest flicker in Ned's direction as she scribbled her address across the top of a spare questionnaire.

25

"Thanks," said Nancy. She tucked the piece of paper inside her purse. "Okay, let's go. Ready, Bess?"

There was no answer. Bess was out cold again.

"Why do you think the doctor's taking so long?" Brad asked nervously as he paced back and forth in the hospital waiting room. "We've been here almost an hour!"

Nancy managed a wan smile. "That's not really long for an emergency room," she said.

Ned spoke up. "I'm sure it's just the flu, anyway," he said. "Bess was probably just on her feet too long, and—"

"Are you waiting for Bess Marvin?" A young, rumpled-looking doctor was standing in the doorway of the waiting room with a clipboard in his hand.

Nancy jumped to her feet. "Yes, we are. How's she doing?"

"Well, we're going to keep her overnight, just to be on the safe side," the doctor said. "Except for a slight rash on her face, her symptoms all point to the flu, but I've ordered some blood samples to be drawn as well. It's just routine," he added. Brad gulped audibly. "Barring anything unusual, she should be released tomorrow morning."

"That's a relief," Nancy said. George and Ned nodded in agreement.

"Can we see her?" asked George.

"For a little while. She should be in her room now." He gave them the room number.

Bess was lying in bed with her eyes half closed. "Hi," she said faintly when she saw her friends. "Sorry to cause so much trouble."

"Oh, Bess, don't say that!" said Nancy. "We're just glad you're okay."

When Bess looked behind Nancy and saw Brad, she stirred restlessly. Her hand moved anxiously to cover her blotchy cheek.

"We'll let you get some rest now," Nancy said quickly. "Call me tomorrow morning, and George and I will come pick you up."

"Have fun tonight," Bess murmured. "Wish I could . . ." She seemed too weak to finish the sentence.

"You just get yourself feeling better," Brad said warmly. "There will be plenty of other nights." Weak though she was, Bess blushed.

As Nancy turned the Mustang onto Heather's street, she had second thoughts about going to Heather's—especially without Ned and George. George had decided to stay at the hospital, and Ned's mom had asked if he couldn't "please" have dinner with them. Still, he would drop by soon, Nancy thought with relief.

I don't even know these kids, Nancy mused, and I'm not sure how I feel about Heather.

27

She's putting the moves on Ned right in front of me!

But something about the group of Emerson students had aroused Nancy's curiosity— some undercurrent of tension that she couldn't exactly define but could feel.

Nancy pulled up in front of Heather's house, parked her car, and walked up the tree-lined walkway to the small ranch-style house. She rang the doorbell. In a second Heather came to the door, wearing a black leather miniskirt and black cashmere sweater.

"Hi," she said unenthusiastically. "Where's Ned?"

Nancy paused for a second. "He'll be coming in a few minutes," she explained.

"Oh, that's good," said Heather, her face brightening. "Everyone else is here," she went on. "Come on in."

Brad, Justin, and Marcia were having sodas and watching a football game on TV in the family room. "How's Bess?" Brad asked immediately. "Have you called the hospital again?"

Nancy had to laugh. "You're as up-to-date on Bess as I am, Brad. I called the hospital just before I came here, and they said she was sleeping. George is having a pretty dull visit."

"They still don't know what's wrong with her?" Marcia asked, trying to sound interested.

"Well, the blood-test results aren't in yet," Nancy answered. "But they don't think it's anything—"

The doorbell rang, interrupting Nancy. Heather jumped to her feet and raced to the door. "Hi, Ned!" they heard her saying happily.

In a second Heather was back in the room, pulling Ned along with her. "See, everyone's here," she said quickly. "Let me show you the rest of the house, okay?" She dragged Ned out of the room before he had time to answer.

"Wait!" protested Justin. "What about the pizza?"

"Oh, you guys go ahead and order it," said Heather casually. "Ned and I will trust you. Won't we, Ned?" She was practically yanking him down the hall. "Come see the living room," she chattered. "It's right in here, and—"

Ned shot a startled glance back at Nancy, but he seemed powerless to stop the flow of Heather's tug.

Marcia stood up quickly. "Nancy and I will order the pizzas," she said. "There's a phone in the kitchen. Come on, Nancy."

"Since when does it take two people to order a pizza?" asked Justin.

"Oh, I want to go with her," said Nancy quickly. From the look in Marcia's eyes, she was sure the other girl wanted to talk to her about something. "I need to get something to drink anyway."

"But you don't know what kind of pizza we want!" Justin complained.

"We'll order plenty," Marcia snapped. "Don't worry about it."

"Okay, but no anchovies!" Justin called after the two girls as they headed out of the family room.

The instant they were in the kitchen, Marcia turned to face Nancy. "I just wanted to warn you that you'd better watch out," she said in a low, intense voice. "Heather has quite a reputation around Emerson for breaking up romances." She raised her voice to a normal level again. "Now, let's see. What kind of pizza do you like?"

"Anything but anchovy," answered Nancy. Lowering her voice, she said, "I wondered if she might have something in mind—but I think I'll be okay."

I certainly don't need any help, she added silently.

Marcia scowled. "Don't be so sure of that," she said.

"Oh, I'll be careful," said Nancy lightly. "Now, let's order. I'm starving." She picked up a phone book from a little table and flipped through it looking for the Yellow Pages.

For a second Marcia stood watching her.

"Well, don't say I didn't warn you," she said, and stalked out of the kitchen.

Nancy called the closest pizza place and ordered four large pizzas. Then she walked back into the family room.

Ned was on the sofa now, Heather next to him—much too close—talking brightly and smiling up at him. But Ned didn't look as though he was enjoying the attention. As Nancy stood there in the doorway, she saw Heather give Ned a little pat on the cheek. He smiled politely and tried to move away from her.

I'm putting a stop to this right now! Nancy told herself.

She walked over to the other side of Ned and sat down firmly. As she did, she thought she heard Ned sigh with relief. He slid his arm behind her shoulders, and Nancy leaned up against him.

Heather scowled and turned away. "When's the pizza coming?" she asked in a sulky voice.

"About twenty minutes," Nancy replied.

"We've been talking about the Halloween party," Ned told her. "Heather was saying she thought we should dress like characters from movies."

Justin was sitting on the floor, stuffing handful after handful of popcorn into his mouth. "That's right," he said barely intelligibly. He gave a big swallow and added, "I'm coming as the shark in *Jaws*. What about you, Brad?"

31

"I haven't made up my mind yet," said Brad. "And when I do, I'm not telling anyone. Aren't these things supposed to be a secret?"

Marcia tipped her head to one side and gave Brad a long look. "Brad could always be Dracula," she suggested. "He seems to go for a different girl every night."

The goad couldn't have been more obvious, but Brad didn't flinch. He hardly even glanced in Marcia's direction, but Heather glared at Marcia.

"Have you picked a costume yet?" Nancy asked Heather, to cover the uneasy silence. There, she thought. No one can say I'm ignoring my hostess.

Heather shook her head. "Not yet, but there's a great costume store in Chicago. I may try there." She turned to Ned. "Want me to get you one, too?"

Nancy's eyes widened. How rude—and how obvious—could Heather be?

But Ned didn't take the bait. "I think I've got one at home," he said pleasantly. "Thanks anyway."

"Oh, no!" Nancy said with a laugh. She was determined not to let Heather get to her. "You're not going to wear that alien invader costume again, are you?"

Justin let out a loud, nervous laugh and knocked over the bowl of popcorn. "Whoops," he said, mugging clownishly. "You know me—

old butterfingers." As he began to scoop up the popcorn, Nancy noticed that his hands were shaking.

What is going on here? she asked herself. Justin's a nervous wreck, Brad's totally ignoring Marcia, and Marcia is obviously trying to torment him.

Brad's voice broke into Nancy's thoughts. "I bet the pizza guy will be here any minute," he said. "Does anyone want to wait for him with me? Justin?"

"Too cold out there," said Justin. "Besides, I'd be too far away from the popcorn."

"Nancy?" asked Brad.

Marcia gave a brittle laugh. "Why should Nancy want to go anywhere with you? I mean, look what happened to her friend. Bess was literally sick of you after only a couple of hours!"

This time Marcia's goad hit home. Brad's face paled. Marcia gave a sly little grin. Then the phone rang, breaking the tension.

"I'll get it," Heather said quickly, and she dashed out of the room. In seconds she was back. "Nancy, it's for you," she said. "It's George."

With an anxious glance at Ned, Nancy walked to the kitchen and picked up the receiver. "Hi, George. How's Bess?"

"She's still asleep," George reported, "but the doctor got the results of the tests."

"So soon?" Nancy asked expectantly.

"Yes," George agreed heavily, "but it's not good."

Nancy gripped the receiver. She forced her voice to stay calm. "Why? What were the results?" she asked.

"There's no doubt about it," said George. "Nancy, Bess—Bess was poisoned!"

Chapter

Four

"POISONED!" NANCY GASPED. She pulled out a kitchen chair and sank into it, shocked. "You mean food poisoning, don't you?"

"No," George replied. "The doctor eliminated that right away. He said the symptoms were all wrong. If Bess had eaten something bad, she'd be sick to her stomach."

"But then that must mean—"

Before Nancy could go on, Justin stuck his head into the kitchen. "Pizza's here!" he blared. "Stop gabbing and get in the family room!"

"I'll be right there!" Nancy said brightly,

putting on a big smile for his benefit. Then she turned back to the phone.

"I don't want anyone to overhear me," she murmured. "So what you're telling me is that someone actually poisoned Bess?"

"Isn't it horrible?"

"Does the doctor know what poison it was?" asked Nancy.

"Not yet," answered George. "It was some kind of chemical, but they haven't been able to identify it."

"I—I can't understand this!" whispered Nancy. "Who would want to hurt Bess?"

George's voice was grim. "I don't know. But we've got to find out."

"I'm going to," Nancy said. "Believe me, I'm going to." She said it to reassure herself as much as George.

I can't go out there right away, Nancy thought after she'd hung up. I need to think about this for a second.

She stared, unseeing, at the opposite wall. The poison must have been in something Bess had eaten or drunk. But what could that have been? They'd been so busy at the mall they hadn't even taken a lunch break. A couple of the kids had grabbed a fast sandwich, and they'd all shared a bag of cookies—but Nancy remembered Bess saying her throat hurt too much to swallow.

The lemonade! Bess had been the only one

to have lemonade. The rest of them had all drunk sodas!

But why would anyone want to poison Bess?

Slowly Nancy pushed back her chair and stood up. As she walked into the family room, Brad looked up.

"Was that George?" he asked instantly. Nancy nodded silently.

"What's wrong, Nancy?" Brad asked. There was a worried look in his eyes. "Don't tell me it's bad news."

Everyone stopped eating to stare at Nancy, and a little warning bell went off in her mind.

I can't tell them about this! she thought. Not until I've eliminated the chance that one of them is the poisoner!

"No, it's not bad news," said Nancy. Brad breathed a sigh of relief. "Bess is feeling much better," Nancy went on. "I guess I just got a little sad thinking of her in the hospital when we're all having fun here." She raised her voice gaily. "Hey, where's that pizza? There's got to be one piece left!"

"Here's some." Justin held the box out to her, and Nancy pulled out a slice.

Nancy took a tiny bite of her pizza and shuddered. Eating was the last thing she wanted to do now.

"How's the game going?" Nancy asked lightly, gesturing toward the TV.

"We're losing." Brad's attention immediately went back to the game.

A while later Heather sighed very loudly. "I should really be upstairs studying. I just know I'm going to fail this course."

"Oh, you're not going to fail," Justin said. "You don't do badly, considering that I've never even seen you crack a book."

"That's because I've got such nice people to help me." Heather smiled at Ned, but to Nancy's relief, Ned didn't smile back. He just looked uncomfortable.

Heather's lips pursed in a definite pout. "Anyway, I'm tired," she said, not too gently nudging them to leave. "Don't you think we should call it quits for tonight? I mean, we have to be at the mall again tomorrow morning."

Justin got to his feet and groaned. "Boy, did I eat too much! Oh, well, I'll work it off tomorrow, filling out all those questionnaires."

Marcia, Ned, and Brad were standing up now, too. Nancy wished she were leaving with Ned; she really wanted to talk to him about all this. It was doubly frustrating since Heather had tried to occupy him all evening.

Not that I'm worried about the competition, Nancy thought. But I would like the chance to spend a little time alone with Ned. . . .

Nancy opened her purse to take out her car keys. As she did, she noticed Justin's gold pen gleaming at the bottom of the purse.

"Oh, Justin, I forgot to return this," she said, pulling out the pen and handing it to him. "Sorry."

"No problem. If you want, you're welcome to keep it and do all the questionnaires tomorrow."

Nancy laughed. "No, I think I'll leave that to you."

"Speaking of leaving—" Ned took a step toward the door, too. "I'd better get home. Great party, Heather."

"It was wonderful having you." This time there was no doubt in Nancy's mind what Heather's comment meant.

Nancy squeezed past Ned and Heather and walked out to her car, but as she started to open the door, she felt a warm hand cover hers.

"I thought I wouldn't get out of there alive!" he muttered. "Can we go out for a soda or something, Nan? I feel as if I haven't gotten the chance to talk to you all day."

Nancy beamed at him. "That's the way I feel, too," she said. "I'll follow you to Fraley's —we can get a soda there."

After a short drive Ned and Nancy pulled up at Fraley's Restaurant, a late-night place. After they were seated, Nancy broke the news about Bess.

"Poison?"

"That's right," Nancy said. "I can hardly believe it, either. My only clue so far is the lemonade," she said. "But who poisoned it or why has me stumped. The only people who touched it, besides the Florida Fresh employees, were Brad and Marcia. And if I had to put money on one of them, it would be Marcia."

"But why?" Ned looked startled.

"Didn't you see how jealous Marcia was of Bess?" Nancy asked.

"Yes, but she couldn't be that jealous!" Ned said blankly. "To poison someone she'd just met—I don't know—it's just not possible, Nancy."

Nancy sighed. "None of this is possible! The only thing that seems likely to me is that the lemonade contained the poison. I plan to check with the Florida Fresh stand tomorrow morning and try to get a sample of that batch of lemonade. Maybe they kept some around."

Ned put his hand on Nancy's. "That's my Nan," he said. "River Heights's best detective. Tell you what. I'll meet you at the mall when it opens. Let's see—tomorrow's Sunday, so it won't be open until eleven. We can go check out Florida Fresh together."

Nancy picked up his hand and held it to her

cheek for a second. "One more Nickerson visit being ruined by a case," she said sadly.

"Oh, it's not ruined at all," said Ned. "I think of it as more time I can spend with you."

Nancy looked at her watch for the twentieth time, then compared it to the large clock in the center of the mall. The results were the same. Her watch wasn't fast. It was Ned who was late.

He must have overslept, Nancy told herself. He wouldn't have forgotten. But if he doesn't get here soon, the others will, and then how are we going to keep this secret?

The two of them had agreed not to mention Bess's poisoning until they knew whether the lemonade was the cause. The marketing group was tense enough.

Nancy decided she'd better give Ned a call. If he had overslept, he'd be upset at not being woken.

Keeping an eye out for Ned, she walked quickly toward the bank of pay phones at the other end of the mall. She passed the Spotless booth on the way. No one from the group had arrived yet.

Or had someone? Wasn't that Marcia standing at one of the phones down there?

It was. Her back was to Nancy, and her whole body was so tense that she looked as

41

though she were about to snap. She was talking so loudly that Nancy couldn't help overhearing.

"I'm warning you," Marcia shouted into the phone. "This is your last chance. Do it now, or I'll tell everyone what you've done!"

Chapter
Five

BEFORE NANCY COULD TAKE another step, Marcia slammed the receiver onto the hook and whirled around. Her face was an ugly mask of anger, and her blue eyes were flashing. Furiously, she began to stride away.

Then she caught sight of Nancy—and instantly her expression changed.

"Oh—uh, hi, Nancy!" she said, with the least convincing smile Nancy had ever seen. "Sorry I almost knocked you down like that, but I'm in a hurry. I've—I've got to go home right away."

"What's the matter?" Nancy asked, pretending not to have heard what Marcia had said.

"Why should anything be the matter?" Marcia asked quickly. "There's nothing wrong. I just realized that I left the questionnaires at home—that's all! I need to hurry back and get them."

Without waiting for Nancy's reply, Marcia rushed toward the mall exit.

I wonder if I should follow her, Nancy thought. I'd bet anything that's not the real reason she got out of here so—

"Nancy! Over here!" Ned's voice carried the entire length of the mall. He was standing under the clock, just where they'd agreed to meet the night before. Nancy walked quickly over to him.

"Sorry I'm late," Ned said, giving her a quick kiss. "I stopped at Justin's house on the way over, and it took longer than I thought."

"What did?"

"I had a brainstorm last night," Ned explained. "I decided to see if Justin still had his old chemistry equipment. I knew you'd want to start checking the lemonade right away, and I figured he'd be the one person we could get to do it today. I didn't tell him why, though. Hope I didn't make a mistake."

"No, it sounds like a great idea!" Nancy said. "Can Justin do the tests?"

"He told me it would take only a few minutes," said Ned. "We agreed he'd try the tests as soon as possible."

"Good," Nancy said. "I talked to Bess this morning, and they're going to let her out of the hospital around noon. George is spending the morning over there, and I'll pick them both up at lunchtime."

"Great," Ned said. "I'm really glad Bess is well enough to leave. By the way, I didn't mention anything about Bess to Justin, and I told him not to say anything about testing the lemonade to anyone else in the group."

"Especially not Marcia." Quickly Nancy described the encounter she'd just had with Marcia. "It may have been perfectly innocent," she said, "but Marcia looked so guilty when she saw me!"

Ned was frowning. "I don't believe in coincidences any more than you do," he said. "We can't dismiss any possibility. Why don't we talk to the Florida Fresh people now? After that, you can tackle Marcia."

"If there is anything in the lemonade, we'll have to tell the police," Nancy said. "But I don't think it's necessary to tell them about the lemonade unless we find something."

"Won't the police have been notified already by the hospital?" Ned asked.

"Probably," Nancy said, racing for the juice bar.

The proprietors of the Florida Fresh stand were an elderly couple named Anderson. They listened carefully as Nancy explained about Bess's poisoning.

"How awful!" said Mrs. Anderson when Nancy had finished. "I'm so sorry for your friend!"

"But you have no real reason for thinking our lemonade was poisoned, do you?" put in her husband testily. "We sold gallons of the stuff yesterday, and no one else has complained. If something had been wrong, we'd have heard about it. I think your friend must've eaten something that didn't agree with her."

"Of course that is a possibility," Nancy said tactfully. She didn't want to rile him.

"It's a certainty, young lady," said Mr. Anderson crisply.

"But maybe the other people ordered lemonade after Bess, and you just haven't been told," Nancy suggested.

"Or maybe they ate so many different things that they couldn't be sure what caused the problem," added Ned.

"Impossible. There is nothing wrong with our lemonade," said Mr. Anderson. He poured himself a glass and took a big swallow. "You see? I have no fears!"

"And I don't think you need to," said Nancy emphatically. "Believe me, I'm not trying to cause trouble. I just want to explore every possibility."

"Of course you do, honey," put in Mrs. Anderson. "Here, let me give you some of the powder. It's from the same carton we used yesterday. Would that be helpful?"

"It certainly would," said Nancy.

Mrs. Anderson poured a cup of the lemonade mix into a plastic bag and sealed it carefully. "Will you let us know what you find out?" she asked.

"I sure will," said Nancy. "That's the least I can do. Thank you both so much."

"What do you think?" Ned asked as they walked away.

"I don't know," Nancy said, biting her lower lip. "But once Justin's analyzed this"—she held up the bag of powder—"we'll know more."

"Perfect timing!" Heather called to Ned and Nancy as they walked toward the booth. Heather, Justin, and Brad were bustling around setting things up. "We just got here a few seconds ago."

Heather's smile was as inviting as it had been the night before, and once again Nancy felt annoyed. Ned had made it clear that he wasn't interested in Heather. Why on earth didn't she give up?

"Our timing could have been even better," Ned countered. "If we'd been about ten minutes later, you guys would have finished by now."

He ducked, laughing, as Brad hurled a sample bottle of Spotless at him. "Just for that, you can set up the display this morning," Brad told him. "Justin and I will supervise."

Nancy bent down to pull the box of supplies from under the table. "Where are the questionnaires?" she asked Heather.

"Oh, I think Marcia took them home yesterday."

Nancy held back her surprise. Maybe Marcia hadn't been lying after all. But if she'd been telling the truth, why had she been so upset on the phone?

It was only five minutes later that Marcia arrived—with a big envelope tucked under her arm and a big smile on her face.

"Sorry I'm late," she said. She didn't look in Nancy's direction, and Nancy didn't say anything.

Marcia pulled a sheaf of blank questionnaires out of the envelope. "Maybe I'm being lazy, but I hope we don't get too many people here today. I don't want to compile all those results."

Heather chuckled. "I'm glad that's not my job, Marcia. I'd never get it done."

"What do you do with the questionnaires?" Nancy asked Marcia. She could hardly believe that the relaxed, smiling girl in front of her was the same one she'd heard on the phone earlier.

"Oh, it's much too boring to describe," said

Marcia with a grin. "Let's talk about something more interesting—like you. How did you meet Ned, anyway?"

Heather had been sitting at the end of the table, talking to the boys, but at Marcia's question she whirled around. "Yes, I was wondering that, too," she said. Somehow Heather's tone managed to come off insulting, as though she couldn't possibly imagine how Nancy had pulled it off.

Nancy smiled, remembering the first time she'd really noticed Ned. "I was on a case," she said.

"A *case?*"

Ned stood up and joined the conversation. "Didn't I tell you that Nancy's a detective? She's pretty famous in River Heights. I guess you've all been away at school a little too long to have heard of her."

"What kind of cases do you solve?" Justin asked excitedly. "Have you ever investigated a murder? Come on, spill the beans! I've never met a detective before!"

"Before you start your story," Brad interjected, "could you tell me how Bess is? Have you heard anything about her?"

Thank goodness! A change of subject, Nancy thought. She never liked talking about her cases. Besides, if one of this group was the poisoner, she wanted to keep a low profile.

"I talked to Bess this morning," Nancy said.

"And she's much better. In fact, she expects to be released around noon."

"That's great!" Brad said delightedly. "Now she'll be able to come to the party—"

"Excuse me. Can someone tell me the ingredients in this?" A pretty brunette had come up to the booth and picked up a jar of Spotless. "I'm allergic to so many things that I have to be careful."

Heather stared blankly at her. "I have no idea," she said. She turned to Marcia. "Do you?"

Marcia shook her head.

"Maybe I can help," said Brad quickly. "I don't know the whole list of ingredients for sure, but I do know that they're all specially selected to be nonallergenic. Only one person out of a hundred thousand will have a reaction to Spotless," he said.

The girl smiled. "You've convinced me. Can I have two jars?"

"I'm really sorry," said Brad. "We can only give out one to a customer. You see, we're doing a survey, and—"

In just a couple of seconds he and the dark-haired girl were deep in conversation.

"Brad's a pretty fast worker," Justin remarked under his breath.

"He seems to be," Nancy agreed. "He sure knows his stuff about Spotless, though."

"Well, he should," said Justin. "There was

an intercollegiate chemistry contest we both entered in our freshman year. Guess who got first prize?" he asked wryly. "It wasn't Justin Dodd, for sure. Brad won, and he wasn't even planning to major in chemistry the way I was." He shook his head. "I swear, some guys have all the luck."

Nancy was just about to ask him more about the contest when she saw a familiar figure running toward her.

"What's George doing here?" she asked in surprise. "She's supposed to be at the hospital with Bess!"

As George approached, Marcia stuck a jar of Spotless in her face.

"Could I interest you in a sample of the best blemish cream you've ever seen?" Marcia suggested jokingly. "You'll be amazed how—"

But at the sight of George's face, Marcia dropped the act. "What is it, George?"

"Yes, what's wrong?" asked Nancy.

"I was just at the hospital," George said, panting. "Five more people have been admitted. And they all have the same symptoms as Bess!"

Chapter

Six

ONLY NED AND NANCY KNEW how serious George's words were.

"Wow, I guess that flu must really be catching," said Heather. "You don't think any of us will get it, do you?"

"It's not the flu!" George burst out before Nancy could stop her. "The doctors ran the same tests, and in all five cases the poison was the same as Bess's!"

"*Poison!*" Heather's voice was almost a shriek. "Bess was poisoned?"

"Nancy, did you know this?" Brad asked. Nancy nodded. "Why didn't you tell me?" Brad burst out.

"We didn't want to worry anyone," Nancy said, not wanting to make George feel bad for telling. "Not until we knew more."

"Oh, Nancy," George said apologetically. "I guess I put my foot in it this time."

"It doesn't matter anymore," said Nancy. "Now that six people are involved, this is a whole new kind of case anyway."

She let out a sigh of relief. At least no one in this group had a grudge against Bess.

Quickly she explained to Ned's friends what had really happened. When she finished, there was an appalled silence.

"What kind of poison is it?" asked Brad at last. "Do the doctors or police know?"

George shook her head. "They don't know what kind it is, or who's doing it, or why. Their theory is that some crazy person is contaminating a common food or drink."

"Like lemonade," Justin said flatly.

"Right," Nancy told him. "That's why we want you to test that powder." There was no reason to keep it a secret any longer. Since more people than Bess had been poisoned, it looked as if none of the Emerson kids was involved.

Brad looked even more horrified than before. "You mean Bess got poisoned from the lemonade I got her? Then that means it's my fault she's sick!" He groaned and put his head in his hands.

"No, it's not!" Nancy said hastily. "Don't feel that way, Brad. For one thing, we have no idea whether or not the poison was in the lemonade. That's why Justin's testing it. Besides, Brad, she's okay now."

George checked her watch. "In fact, Nancy, you and I should head over there to get her."

"And I'll test that lemonade," said Justin. "Ned, do you want to come along and help?"

"Sure," said Ned. "Will the rest of you be okay without us?"

Marcia spoke up. "I'm sure we will. The crowds aren't nearly as bad as they were yesterday. In fact, I think I'll even go home for a late lunch. No more mall food for me!"

Nancy and George headed out of the mall and got into Nancy's Mustang. On the way to the hospital, they discussed the case but came up blank. Nancy decided that once they were at the hospital she wanted to question the other poisoning victims to see if there was any common thread.

When Nancy and George arrived at the hospital, they found Bess still in bed. "I'm not ready!" she wailed at the sight of the girls. "I haven't put on my makeup yet."

Nancy chuckled. "Glad to see you're feeling better, anyway. How long do you think it'll take you to get ready?"

"Only twenty minutes, I swear," said Bess.

Twenty minutes, Nancy thought. That will probably be enough time. "George, would you keep Bess company?" she asked. George nodded, and Nancy headed out of Bess's room.

One of the nurses on duty gave Nancy the names and room numbers of the five other people who had been poisoned. "You're in luck," she added. "Visiting hours have just started."

The first name on the list was Bonnie Harte. She'd been the first person after Bess to be admitted with the same symptoms. Nancy knocked on her door, and a cheery voice called, "Come in!"

Nancy opened the door to find a pretty teenage girl with short black hair and elfin features.

"I'm Nancy Drew," she told Bonnie. "I'm a private detective, and I'm investigating this poisoning. Would you mind answering a few questions?"

Bonnie shook her head. "It'd be great to have someone to talk to. Being here is boring."

In answer to Nancy's first question, Bonnie said she was a junior at River Heights High. "That's where I went, too," Nancy told her with a smile.

"I thought you looked familiar!" Bonnie said, then frowned. "But I'm sure I've seen you recently, though," she said thoughtfully. "You weren't at the mall yesterday, were you?"

"As a matter of fact, I was," said Nancy. "So you were there, too? Did you have anything to eat or drink there?"

"Nope," Bonnie replied. "I went right after lunch so I wouldn't be tempted by the ice-cream stand. I'm going to be a mermaid for Halloween, and I have to fit into my costume."

Strike one, thought Nancy.

She said goodbye and went down the hall checking in on the other poison victims. Douglas Brody was a ruddy-cheeked football player whose only worry was how long he'd have to miss practice. Tiffany Weld was so sleepy that she kept dropping off in the middle of her sentences. Maryanne Jansen was fussing about all the homework she'd have to make up. And Todd Leithauser described his symptoms in such graphic detail that Nancy couldn't wait to get away.

None of the poison victims had had lemonade. The only thing they had in common besides their symptoms was the fact that they were all students at River Heights High.

"Bess, if only you were still in school, I'd have a link," Nancy said back in Bess's hospital room. "Maybe you're the exception, though," she mused. Maybe the other poison cases are linked. Could there be something going on at the school?"

"I always said the cafeteria food was poisonous," George quipped.

Both Nancy and Bess groaned.

"Speaking of food," Nancy said, "do either of you feel like getting some lunch? I was just about to call Ned and ask him to meet me somewhere. I want to find out what Justin's tests showed."

"Not today," Bess said. "After this, I can't even think about food."

"I don't believe it!" George's eyes widened in surprise. "This is one for the record books. Bess Marvin just refused food!"

"Nancy, can you drop us off at my house?" Bess asked. "I know my parents are anxious for me to get home."

"Let's go," Nancy said, smiling. "I'm glad you're back among the living, Bess."

As she parked her Mustang in the Mexican restaurant's parking lot, Nancy saw both Justin and Ned waiting for her by the front door.

"Can you join us for lunch, Justin?" Nancy asked.

Justin pushed his sunglasses up on top of his head. "No way. I ate enough junk food last night," he said ruefully. "I just wanted to give you the results of the test. Or, rather, the lack of results. Nancy, I tried every test I know, but there was no poison in that lemonade."

"Well, now that I've talked to the other five victims, I was expecting that," Nancy told him. "Bess is the only one who drank lemonade. I guess that rules out Florida Fresh. At least the Andersons will be happy when I tell them. Thanks anyway, Justin."

"Happy to oblige," he said. "I love mucking around with chemicals."

When she and Ned were seated in their booth, Nancy filled him in on her talk with the five other poison victims at the hospital. "All I can think is that there's something going on at River Heights High," she finished. "Either that, or—"

She stopped. "Or?" Ned prompted her.

"Well, I suddenly thought of another theory, but it sounds crazy," said Nancy slowly.

Ned's smile was reassuring. "Nancy, I've seen you on a lot of cases, and when your instincts tell you something, they're usually right. So what's your latest hunch?"

"Well, do you remember the sleeping pill scare a few years ago, when someone put cyanide in the pills?" asked Nancy.

"Sure, I remember."

Nancy paused. "I just wonder if maybe this couldn't be the same thing. Maybe the doctors are wrong about the poison being in food or drink. Maybe it was in a medicine."

"You could be right," Ned said slowly, a new idea dawning on him. "Bess wasn't feeling well even before she drank the lemonade."

"That's what got me thinking about it. I wonder if she took anything for her sore

58

throat. I'll call her as soon as we get back to the mall. Did you have fun helping Justin?" Nancy asked.

"I had fun, but I didn't help—he had everything under control. You know, it was weird—when I watched Justin do those tests, I couldn't figure out why he'd dropped chemistry. He's really good!"

"That's not what he says," Nancy replied. "He told me he switched majors because he wasn't good enough. But maybe Justin doesn't do anything unless he can be the best at it—no matter how many jokes he cracks."

Ned nodded. "I can vouch for that. You should see him in this marketing class. He's the top student every time. I'm sure he'll be the one to get the job with the ad agency."

"How about Heather?" Nancy asked, trying not to let any cattiness creep into her voice. "How does she do?"

Ned winced. "She just sort of coasts along, but not badly actually. Grades aren't exactly the main thing on her mind. Now, if an ad agency offered a job in the Stealing Guys from Their Girlfriends Department—"

"Just as long as it doesn't work with you," Nancy told him.

"You've got to be kidding!" Ned exclaimed. "Heather? Nancy, that's an insult to my good judgment."

"Okay, okay," Nancy said with a laugh. "I

don't want to start sounding like Marcia. And speaking of Marcia, I'd like to talk to her. Something about that phone call doesn't make sense."

"Why don't we go talk to her now?" Ned asked. "She went home for lunch."

Nancy checked her watch. "Good idea. Do you have her address, Ned?"

"I sure do. I even know how to get to her house. Let's drive there together in my car."

The trip to Marcia's was short, and Ned and Nancy easily found her street. As Ned turned the wheel to pull onto her block, he was stopped by a police car blocking the intersection.

"What's going on?" Nancy wondered aloud. She rolled down her window and called to the officer in the car, "Can we go through here?"

"Where are you headed?" he asked in return.

"To visit a friend," Nancy replied. "Marcia Grafton."

The officer just stared at her instead of replying.

"I think she lives down at the end of the—" Ned began, but the officer cut him off.

"Would you please park your car and come with me?" he asked them politely.

"Why?" asked Nancy. "What's wrong?"

The man did not answer. He just gestured again to the side of the road.

A feeling of dread swept over Nancy as she and Ned got out of the car. Something was wrong—very wrong.

As they followed the officer toward another squad car, Nancy spotted a familiar figure.

"Chief McGinnis!" she called. She had worked with the chief on earlier cases. "Maybe he'll tell us what's going on," she said to Ned in a low voice.

Chief McGinnis turned and stared at her. "Nancy, are you here to investigate?" he asked.

"Investigate what?"

Now the chief's expression was grim. "There's a young woman on this street who's very sick."

Nancy grabbed Ned's hand.

"Who is it?" she asked.

But she didn't need to ask the question. She knew the answer before Chief McGinnis had opened his mouth. His words only confirmed her worst fears.

"Marcia Grafton."

Chapter

Seven

WHAT HAPPENED TO HER?" Nancy asked, her eyes wide.

"We're not really sure," Chief McGinnis replied. "But we'll know when we get the report from the hospital. By the time the rescue squad had arrived, Marcia was unconscious."

Nancy and Ned exchanged a glance. Marcia's collapse sounded frighteningly familiar.

"You don't seem too shocked," the chief commented. Then, staring hard at Ned, he asked, "Who's your friend?"

"Ned?" Nancy asked, surprised. "This is my boyfriend, Ned Nickerson, Chief."

She stopped when she caught sight of the other police officer's raised eyebrows. He looked down at the top sheet of paper on a clipboard and nodded at the chief.

"Would you two please get into the back seat?" Chief McGinnis asked. He made a quick gesture toward his car and wouldn't meet Nancy's startled eyes.

"Tell me about your relationship with Marcia Grafton," the chief said abruptly when Nancy and Ned were in the back seat.

He can't suspect me of anything! Nancy thought in amazement. He knows me!

Ned was speaking now in a calm and measured voice. "She's a classmate of mine," he explained. "We were working on a special research project at the mall."

The chief's face was expressionless. It was impossible for Nancy to guess what he was thinking. "Who else is working on the project?" he asked.

Ned gave him the names, and Chief McGinnis jotted quick notes on his clipboard, comparing his notes to the sheet of paper the other officer had left with him. Nancy tried to catch a glimpse of that sheet, but the wire mesh separating the front and back seats made it impossible.

"How about you, Nancy?" the chief asked in an expressionless voice. "What's your connection here?"

Nancy steadied her nerves. What was going on? "I was helping Ned and the rest of the group," she said.

Chief McGinnis made another note. "If your project was at the mall, why were you going to Marcia's house?" Again there was just a hint of suspicion in his voice.

"She was eating lunch at home, and I wanted to ask her a few questions."

"Oh, so you *are* investigating this case?" the chief said instantly.

"Well, I— In a way I am, yes. You see, my friend Bess was—"

Before Nancy could finish, the other police officer opened the front door of the squad car and climbed inside. "No change in her condition," he said.

"How sick *is* Marcia?" asked Nancy.

"Very," said Chief McGinnis tersely. "The last report from the hospital was that she's in a coma."

"A coma! But she was fine two hours ago!" Nancy gasped.

"Well, she's not anymore," answered the chief.

"Was she at home when you found her?" asked Nancy.

"Yes. She was lying on the kitchen floor not far from the phone," the other officer added. "She looked as if she were about to have lunch. The table was set, and there was a half-full glass of soda at her place."

The police radio squawked, and Chief McGinnis picked up the receiver.

"We've got the others," a woman's voice said. "We're on our way to HQ."

"Good work," said the chief. "So are we."

He turned to Nancy and Ned. "You'll have to come to headquarters with us. We need to take some statements." He gave them a long, appraising look, as though he were trying to decide something. Then he added, "You can take your own car."

Nancy and Ned got back into Ned's car. Chief McGinnis drove off, Ned following.

"A coma!" Nancy exclaimed as she and Ned drove toward the center of River Heights. "I can't believe it!"

Ned's face was taut and white. "I can't, either. And I wonder just how the police think we're connected to all this."

"I wish I could have seen what was on that piece of paper they both kept looking at," said Nancy.

"I don't like this, Nan," Ned added grimly. "Not at all."

They were pulling up in front of the police

station now. Ned parked, and he and Nancy quickly scooted up the wide concrete steps past flocks of scurrying pigeons.

The hallway seemed dim after the bright sunshine. Nancy and Ned followed the two officers through a maze of corridors.

Chief McGinnis ushered them into a small room at the end of one hall.

"What are you guys doing here?"

It was Justin. He, Heather, and Brad were sitting on gray metal folding chairs in the room. All of them looked a little sick.

"Probably the same thing as you," Ned answered with a wry smile.

"Sit down, Nancy and Ned," the chief said. When they were seated, he began talking.

"We have a serious case of poisoning on our hands, and I understand that all of you knew the victim. As you may be aware, there's been a rash of poisonings in the River Heights area over the past two days. Your friend has the same symptoms as the others—only hers are far worse. Now, I'd like each of you to tell me where you were today."

"You mean, after we closed down the booth?" asked Heather in a trembling voice. "Because, you know, Marcia said we might as well close it since there weren't any customers, so we—"

"After you closed down the booth," the

chief cut in. "After the group broke up, and you were on your own."

Brad flinched. Justin's gulp was audible, and Heather squeezed her hands together so tightly her knuckles turned white.

"You want our alibis." There was a tremor in Justin's voice.

Chief McGinnis nodded. "That's one way of describing it."

"I might as well start," Justin volunteered. "I was at my house in River Heights with Ned."

"Doing what?"

Justin bit his lip. "I was doing a chemistry test," he said.

"A chemistry test?" Chief McGinnis raised his head and stared at Justin. "What kind of chemistry test?" he asked.

Once again Justin hesitated, and Nancy felt a surge of sympathy for him. She knew how incriminating his next statement was going to sound.

Ned cleared his throat. "We were testing lemonade for poison," he said.

I've got to explain! Nancy thought. "Chief, my friend Bess was one of the people poisoned yesterday," she said. "I thought she might have drunk tainted lemonade. That's why Ned asked Justin to test the mix."

"I know a lot about chemistry," began Justin. Then he stopped short. "That makes it sound as though— Well, you see—"

"I see," said the chief dryly. "I'm going to need to talk to you privately. Can you corroborate his statement?" he asked Ned.

Ned nodded, and Chief McGinnis turned to Nancy. "Where were you?"

"I was helping Bess Marvin check out of the hospital." Nancy's voice was steady. She knew that the hospital records would include the time of discharge. The police would be able to verify her statement. "Then I went to a restaurant to meet Ned. The waitress can vouch for us."

"I was shopping at the mall," Heather said when it was her turn.

The officer raised his eyebrows quizzically. "That's not going to be easy to prove," he said.

"Did you buy anything?" Nancy asked quickly.

Heather nodded, but her face was pale and her hands were trembling. "I did get a sweater, but I returned it about fifteen minutes later," she said. "But maybe the salesgirl could—"

"We'll check into it," said the chief briskly. He turned to Brad. "How about you?"

"I was shopping, too. My mom's birthday is this week." Brad's voice was firm, almost defiant. "I didn't buy anything, though, if that's your next question."

"Well, that's all the questions I have—for

now, anyway," said Chief McGinnis. "I'll have
these statements typed and ready for your
signatures in a few minutes. Then you'll be
free to go."

Brad, Justin, Heather, and Ned filed halting-
ly from the room, but Nancy stayed behind.
She had a question of her own—and she
wasn't going to be frightened out of asking it.

"How did you know we all knew Marcia?"
Nancy asked the chief.

"That wasn't hard." The chief pulled a
familiar-looking sheet of paper from his clipboard. It was the one Nancy had tried to read
in the squad car.

"We found this in the victim's house," he
said, and began to read from it.

The sheet was an explanation of the Spotless
marketing project. It listed all the students
who were participating, their addresses, and
the location and dates of the test.

"We also found these," the chief went on.
He pulled a pile of papers out of a large manila
envelope.

They were Spotless questionnaires.

"'Douglas Brody, age eighteen, formerly
used Clearly,'" the chief read aloud. "'Bonnie
Harte, age seventeen, used Clearly—Chuck
Loomis, age fourteen, several different
products—Maryanne Jansen, age sixteen, no
other product—Adam Poulios, age fifteen,
used—'"

"Wait a minute," Nancy interrupted tensely. "This can't be a coincidence. I talked to some of those people this morning! Can I see that list?"

The chief held it out, and Nancy took it. Her hands were trembling with excitement.

"I knew it," she said after a second.

All five poisoning victims she'd met in the hospital were on the list!

Chapter

Eight

"THIS LIST SOLVES *ONE* MYSTERY," Nancy told Chief McGinnis triumphantly. "Every one of the poison victims sampled Spotless."

"Spotless? Isn't that the cream you were testing?" asked the chief.

Nancy nodded. "All five kids I talked to at the hospital this morning took samples of Spotless. Every one of their names is here. That can't possibly be a coincidence!"

When the chief looked at her curiously, Nancy went on. "At first I thought the poisoning must have something to do with River Heights High," she explained. "But if everyone used Spotless, it all fits perfectly!"

Chief McGinnis stared at her thoughtfully. "It certainly makes a lot of sense," he said. "Are you sure Marcia Grafton and your friend Bess both used the cream, too?"

"Bess definitely did," Nancy said, nodding emphatically. "I saw her rub it into her face less than an hour before she fainted. I don't know for sure about Marcia, but I'd guess she'd at least have tried Spotless. She's been giving out samples of it—she must have put it on at some point."

"Enough to send her into a coma, though?" asked the chief.

Nancy paused. "I don't know. You're right —that does sound a little farfetched. Still, I can't believe there isn't a connection between these poisonings and Spotless."

Chief McGinnis nodded slowly. "You may be right, Nancy. There have been cases of product tampering, and this could be one of them. Good thinking on your part." He reached for the phone. As he dialed, he said, "We'll do some tests on your samples and contact the manufacturer."

After he had given a few terse orders to the person on the other end of the line, Chief McGinnis turned back to Nancy.

"We'd better find your friends. Until we've resolved this, your marketing test is officially on hold." He smiled at her ruefully. "We don't want the entire teenage population of River Heights in the hospital."

"Looks like that job with Premier just went down the tubes," Justin said moodily. "I wish we could just dump this stupid booth in a trash can somewhere."

Justin, Brad, Heather, Nancy, and Ned had just come from the police station. They were at the mall now, dismantling the Spotless booth they'd been so proud of just a day earlier. Everyone was feeling irritable.

"I wouldn't give up hope about the job," Ned told Justin. Ned and Nancy were packing the remaining samples of Spotless to take to Chief McGinnis. The police lab would test them and then impound them as evidence. "After all, the people at Spotless will have to realize this wasn't our fault," Ned went on.

"If anything, they'll probably be relieved that we caught this problem before Spotless was actually out on the market," Nancy put in.

"I guess you're right," said Justin, with a faint echo of his old jokey manner. "I mean, a blemish cream that poisons people is a great gimmick, but people would probably get tired of it pretty quickly."

"Do you *have* to joke about this?" Brad burst out angrily. "Two of our friends have just been poisoned, and you think it's funny?"

73

"Of course I don't think it's funny!" Justin snapped. "But what do you want me to do—cry?"

"Stop it, both of you!" said Heather sharply. She had been folding the tablecloth almost mechanically. Now she slapped the tablecloth furiously into its box and glared at Brad and Justin.

"You're both being horrible," she said. "And I don't know about the rest of you, but this is the end for me. I'm dropping out of this stupid marketing program. It's not worth it!"

Brad raised his head from the carton he was loading and stared at Heather for a moment. "That's pretty drastic," he said.

"Tell me poisoning's not drastic!" Heather retorted. "At least seven people are sick, and one of them may not live. If that's not serious, I don't know what is."

Brad pushed the carton shut and stood up. "Well, I don't think you should change your major just because of an accident," he said. "That's the last carton, guys. We're ready to roll."

Without another word they each grabbed a box and started walking toward the mall exit.

Nancy's carton was too heavy for her to walk very fast. She quickly fell to the back of the group behind Justin and Heather. As Nancy watched, Justin touched Heather's arm and drew her aside. He began talking to her in a low voice—and judging from the expression on his face, what he was saying was not pleasant.

I wonder what he's up to, Nancy thought as she passed them, not close enough to hear.

For no particular reason, a memory of the day before floated into her mind. It was the memory of Justin knocking the bottle of Spotless out of Bess's hand.

"That stuff is dangerous!" he had shouted.

He had been right.

Could Justin have tampered with the samples? After all, he had worked for Spotless's main competitor. Maybe he still was. What if he had deliberately sabotaged the samples just to help Asco?

Nancy shivered. It was an ugly thought, and she didn't want to believe it.

But what if the same thought had occurred to Marcia? Nancy suddenly wondered. Maybe Marcia had been threatening Justin on the phone this morning! Perhaps she had realized that he'd tampered with the Spotless samples, tried to blow the whistle on him—and been poisoned to get her out of the way.

There was only one thing to do: find out what Justin was up to. She decided to head out to Asco right away. If I could just get a look at Justin's employee file there, Nancy thought. That would be a good place to start—

"So what do you say, Nancy?" Ned's voice brought her back to the present.

"What? I'm sorry, Ned. I wasn't listening." She set her carton down to rest her arms.

Ned rested his carton on top of hers and ruffled her hair. "Last Night is playing at the War Memorial tomorrow night," Ned said. Last Night was one of his and Nancy's favorite bands. "Do you want to go?"

Ned gestured toward Brad, who was walking alone a few yards ahead of them. "He's taking this pretty hard. Why don't we ask him to go with us? We could invite Bess and make it a double date."

"I think it's a great idea." Nancy gave him a warm smile. "But don't you have to get back to school tomorrow, now that you're not working?"

"Nope. We're excused for the next few days. Might as well take advantage of our time together. Hey, Brad!" Ned said.

Brad, still carrying his carton, turned around to face them. Quickly Ned told him about the concert and invited him to come along. "We're going to ask Bess, too," he said with a conspiratorial grin.

"Perfect!" said Brad. "I need something like this to cheer me up. Besides, there's something I want to talk to you and Nancy about."

"We probably should invite Justin and Heather, too," Nancy said. Ned nodded.

Nancy turned back to look for Justin and Heather—and realized that this was not the time to ask them about a concert.

Heather and Justin were still caught up in their argument. Justin's face was beet red now. Nancy couldn't hear what he was saying, but she could tell that he was furious. Heather looked both frightened and defiant. Her eyes were darting around as if she was looking for a place to escape.

Suddenly she shook her head violently. "No!" she cried. "I said no!" This time Nancy had no trouble understanding her words.

Heather charged headlong toward the mall exit.

Just as quickly Justin dashed after her. In a few steps he'd caught up to her. He grabbed her forearm and pulled her roughly to a stop.

"No!" Heather cried again. As Nancy watched, she wrenched her arm from Justin's grasp.

"Leave me alone, Justin!" she shouted. "I won't do it!"

Chapter

Nine

JUSTIN'S FACE was only inches from Heather's now. As Nancy watched, he raised a fist threateningly and shook it at Heather, who shrank back in terror. Then he smashed his fist into the wall next to her and stormed angrily out the door.

Nancy rushed up to Heather. "Are you okay?" she asked.

With a shaking hand, Heather pushed a lock of hair back into place. Her whole face was twitching. She licked her lips nervously and made a brave attempt at a smile. "Sure," she said. "No problem!"

"What was that all about?" Nancy asked.

"Oh, nothing," Heather said quickly. "Nothing's wrong. Really. Or nothing will be as soon as I get rid of this." She looked down at the shopping bag she was carrying. "I don't ever want to see another test sample or think about another questionnaire. This is definitely not the field for me!"

She began walking out the exit again, and Nancy walked beside her. When they reached Heather's car, Nancy asked, "Are you sure you're all right to drive?"

"Oh, yes," Heather said, but there was still a tremor in her voice. "I'll be fine once I'm out of this stupid mall. Thanks for asking. I—I appreciate it."

There was a look of real gratitude in her eyes. She paused for a second, as if she wanted to say something more. Then she climbed into the car and shut the door.

Nancy stood watching as Heather backed out, and then she tried to find Justin. He had obviously gone. Nancy scanned the parking lot for Ned. He and Brad were leaning against Ned's car, the two cartons piled beside them. They were engrossed in conversation, and Nancy didn't want to interrupt them. She gave them a quick wave as she hopped into her car and pulled out of the parking lot. She'd ask Ned later what was going on with Justin— maybe Brad knew something.

A swift glance at her watch told Nancy she'd

have to hurry if she had any chance at all of getting into Asco on a Sunday. The afternoon was almost over.

Nancy would have enjoyed a leisurely drive over to LeBlond Avenue, where Asco headquarters were. The maples were just turning to their brilliant fall colors, and the sun was just setting. That day, though, Nancy was barely aware of her surroundings. All her thoughts were focused on where she was going—and how she was going to get inside. She had a plan, but she wasn't at all sure it was going to work.

She had driven by the Asco buildings many times before without ever paying much attention to them. Now, as she approached the visitors' parking lot, Nancy realized that the long, low white-brick building in front of the factory must contain Asco's central offices. She parked close to the front door and walked around to the trunk.

Good thing I have my toolbox in the car, she thought as she lifted the trunk door and pulled out the metal box.

Now, if only she could use it to bluff her way inside to find out what she needed to know . . .

Nancy boldly walked up to the front door of the main building. If she was lucky, she'd soon know the truth about Justin Dodd's relationship with Asco. If her luck didn't hold— Nancy didn't want to think about how she'd explain her presence in the Asco executive offices to Chief McGinnis. He'd been understanding in the past, but Nancy doubted that he'd be able to overlook entry under false pretenses.

Gripping her toolbox in one hand, Nancy walked into the building. There, at a large reception desk, sat a guard. She seemed to be the only person around.

The guard was a middle-aged woman in a blue uniform. She was watching her tiny TV so intently that she didn't even notice Nancy walk up to the desk. Nancy had to clear her throat to get the woman's attention.

"I'm here to repair the computer in the personnel office," she told the guard. "They called us yesterday, but this is the first chance we've had to get here."

"Personnel's down the hall, second on the right," the guard said in a bored voice. Clearly she accepted the fact that when an Asco computer was broken, it had to be fixed—even on a Sunday.

Well, that was easier than I expected! Nancy thought. Now all she needed to do was find the file—and hope no one from personnel had decided to work on Sunday.

As she opened the door and switched on the lights, Nancy whistled softly. This was an expensive office! There was an oriental rug on the floor, and the desks were made of highly polished walnut. From the lush potted trees and brass desk accessories to the dark walnut paneling, no expense had been spared. And this was only the personnel office. What could the executive offices be like?

Obviously Asco was a profitable company, or one that wanted to give the impression that it was profitable. But were its profits based on sales of products like Clearly? Or had they been generated by sabotaging a competitor?

That was one of the things Nancy hoped to find out.

She breathed a sigh of relief when she saw personal computers on several of the desks. She switched one on and put her open toolbox next to it. If anyone happened to walk by, it would look as though she were really trying to repair the computer.

As long as no one asks me any questions, Nancy thought.

Her eyes raced around the room, searching for file cabinets. Asco was a big company. The personnel records for its employees would have to be stored in a lot of files.

But there were no files in this main reception room.

Nancy looked again. There had to be files somewhere. Even if most of the employee information was kept on the computer, every personnel department did keep paper files. Where were Asco's?

As she cast her eyes slowly around the room, Nancy saw a gleaming brass doorknob in the middle of one wall of dark paneling. Was this the door to the file room?

Nancy turned the knob, but the door didn't budge. She walked back to her toolbox and pulled out a ring of picks. Opening locked doors was a skill she'd completely mastered. It would take only a few seconds to open this one.

But it didn't.

The lock was a kind she'd never seen before, and it took at least five agonizing minutes before she had the door open. Nancy studied the lock carefully. Unlike most of the locks she'd encountered over the years, this one required a key to open it on both sides.

Nancy flipped on the lights and breathed a sigh of relief. This small, windowless room did hold the files. Three of the four walls were lined with cabinets. A table with a single chair sat in the middle of the room, probably to give the file clerks space to work.

Nancy walked quickly to the files, her eyes scanning the labels for the drawer that would hold Justin's personnel record. There it was— the one with the *D*'s.

She was about to slide it open when she heard footsteps.

Leaving the file-room door open just a crack, Nancy raced back to the outer room and up to the computer with her toolbox next to it. She was staring intently at the computer when the guard stuck her head through the door.

"Any luck?" the guard asked.

Nancy shook her head. "I've run diagnostic tests," she said. "Nothing seems to be wrong."

The guard tut-tutted sympathetically. "There's a soda machine at the end of the hall," she told Nancy. "Want one?"

"No thanks," Nancy said. She waited, listening tensely, until she heard the guard return to her desk. Then she quickly moved back to the file room. Once again she left the door open just a crack. If anyone looked into the personnel department, they'd think the file room was safely closed and locked.

At least that was what Nancy hoped.

She opened the *D* file with a mounting sense of anticipation. There was Justin's section— the one marked "DOB–DOL." In just a few seconds Nancy would know the truth about him!

"'Dodd, Alicia,'" she muttered aloud. "'Dodd, Martin. Doddson'—wait!"

There was no "Dodd, Justin" file.

There had to be! Justin hadn't denied working for Asco. He'd been open about the fact that he'd been a summer intern there. He had to have a personnel file!

Perhaps it was misfiled. Nancy looked carefully through the entire drawer of *D*'s.

The folder wasn't there.

Nancy hadn't been sure what she'd find in the file. She hoped that it would confirm exactly what Justin had told her—that he had worked for Asco during the summer but was no longer on the payroll. She had been afraid that the file would show he was still working for them—that perhaps he was on special assignment to sabotage Spotless. The one thing she hadn't expected was that there wouldn't be a file.

In her disappointment, Nancy closed the file drawer harder than she'd intended. As she did, she heard an ominous click. She turned quickly to see what had happened.

Oh, no! she thought. It couldn't be!

The force of the slamming file drawer had blown the file-room door closed.

Nancy raced to the door and turned the handle frantically—but she was too late. The damage was done. The door had locked, and all her tools were on the other side.

Nancy was trapped inside the Asco file room!

Chapter

Ten

Nancy stared at the door, thinking fast.
She had to get out!

She'd already spent too much time at Asco.
The guard might be more interested in her TV
than in visitors, but eventually she'd start
wondering why it was taking Nancy so long to
repair the computer. Then she'd come looking
for her.

Nancy tried the door again, but she knew it
wouldn't open. It didn't. Nancy cast her eyes
slowly around the room, inspecting every inch.
There must be something in there she could
use to pick the lock.

There wasn't. The room contained only a

single table, a chair, and file cabinets. Besides, Nancy knew nothing short of professional lock picks could get her out.

There were no windows, no other doors. The file room was nothing more than a large closet.

Nancy paced the floor. Then a thought suddenly occurred to her. She looked up—and for the first time since the door had closed, a smile crossed her face. It just might work.

The first step was to move the table up next to the door. Nancy breathed silent thanks that the file-room table was made of lightweight metal rather than solid, heavy wood. It was sturdy enough for what she had in mind, but she could easily push it.

Nancy's heart began to pound as she climbed on top of the table. What if her plan didn't work?

Don't think about that! she told herself sternly. Then, standing on the table, she reached up and tried to touch the ceiling.

It was no good. Stretch though she might, there was still a six-inch gap between her fingertips and the ceiling panels.

Nancy jumped down lightly and lifted the chair onto the table. This would be trickier, but it was the only way to get the height she needed.

She balanced the chair against the wall, then climbed onto it. Now she had no trouble touching the ceiling. With both palms flat, she lifted a ceiling panel and slid it to the side.

She had to swallow a shout of relief. The space was just as she'd hoped!

Like those of most commercial buildings, the Asco offices had dropped ceilings. Removable tiles rested on metal gridworks, which left a two-foot space between them and the plaster ceiling. The space was designed for heating ducts and telephone wires.

It also offered enough room for an escape route.

Nancy carefully hoisted herself into the crawl space and stretched out on her stomach to support her weight. The metal gridwork was strong enough to support the ceiling tiles, but Nancy had no way of knowing whether it would hold her.

Holding her breath, she slid forward an inch at a time toward the other room. There she removed another ceiling tile—and then lowered herself into the room.

Nancy raced to her toolbox, grabbed her lock picks, and opened the door to the file room again. Then she climbed back onto the table, this time to replace the ceiling tiles.

When she was sure that both rooms looked the same as before, Nancy closed the file-room door for the last time.

"Is that dust in your hair?" Ned asked her a little while later. Nancy had called him after leaving Asco, and they'd agreed to meet for a soda. After that, Nancy planned to go home for a late dinner and bed.

She reached up to pat the top of her head. "Could be," she said. "I've been all over since I saw you last." She leaned back against the back of the booth and yawned.

"What do you mean? Where were you?"

Nancy grinned. "Checking out a hunch—the hard way." Quickly she filled him in on her adventure in the Asco personnel offices.

"I can't believe it!" Ned marveled. "You're lucky you didn't get caught!"

Now that it was over, it didn't seem to Nancy as though she'd been in much danger. She shrugged. "The only risky part was jumping down from the ceiling. That's where my judo training was useful. If there's one thing I learned in those classes, it was how to fall softly." She chuckled. "Believe me, Ned—it was a long way down."

"But you didn't find out anything?" he asked.

"That's the strange thing. I don't understand why Justin's file was missing. It makes me wonder if there's some kind of cover-up. Do you suppose Asco really has something to hide?"

"Like what?" Ned asked as the waitress put down their sodas.

"Well, I've been thinking about it. Asco

stands to gain more than anyone if Spotless is discredited," Nancy explained. "Clearly is Spotless's main competitor. If Spotless never makes it to the market, Clearly will keep making a fortune for Asco."

Ned nodded. "I still can't picture Justin being part of something illegal, though," he said. "It just doesn't seem like him."

"You noticed him at the mall this afternoon," Nancy countered. "Even I was scared of him."

Ned's dark eyes looked concerned. "I didn't watch what was happening very closely—I was too busy talking to Brad. I thought Justin and Heather were playing around. They've always been good friends. It isn't that they've dated, but they've been buddies since I've known them. Well, they're under a lot of strain—especially now that Spotless may be causing all this sick mess. I hope McGinnis finds out soon who or what's to blame." Ned paused a moment, then quickly added, "Oh, I dropped our remaining samples off at police headquarters."

"Good. The sooner we know, the better. Heather said she felt down enough to drop out of the program altogether."

Ned looked startled. "Maybe she really does mean it. She always says she's dropping out, but I thought she was just trying to get us to coax her to stay." He shook his head. "I'll say one thing—we all need a break."

"Well, there's always Justin's costume party —if anyone's still speaking, that is," Nancy said with a laugh.

"Do you think we should go?" Ned asked.

"Try to keep me away!" said Nancy. "It'll be the perfect chance to keep an eye on my number one suspect. Besides, I bet you'll look cute in the little bunny costume I got for you. Just kidding! Just kidding!" She squealed as Ned picked up his water glass and tipped it threateningly over her head.

"Watch out, Nancy Drew!" Ned said. "You're skating on thin ice!"

Nancy laughed. Their playfulness was making her feel a lot better. "I have to be getting home. It's late."

"Sure," Ned said, picking up the check and reaching for his wallet.

A few minutes and a kiss from Ned later, Nancy was heading home. When she reached her house, she parked her car in front and hurried up the steps to the front porch. Her father was still out of town with a client, but Nancy knew that Hannah Gruen, the Drews' housekeeper, would be keeping dinner for her, and she didn't want to make Hannah wait.

The porch light wasn't on, so Nancy didn't see anything unusual until she opened the front door and the light from the house spilled onto the porch.

There at the side of the door was a small cardboard box. It had no label—just Nancy's name printed in bold letters.

That's strange, Nancy thought. No one delivers on Sunday.

She picked up the box and opened it carefully. When she saw what was inside, her eyes widened with shock.

There was no mistaking it. Nancy had seen those white plastic containers too many times not to recognize this one. Someone had left her a sample of Spotless.

As she lifted the jar from the box, Nancy saw a card. She turned it over—and when she saw the printing, her face grew pale.

"You're next, Nancy Drew!"

Chapter

Eleven

Nancy kept her cool. She'd gotten anonymous notes like this one often enough in the past. They always meant that someone had a real stake in trying to get her off a case.

She stepped into the house and looked closely at the card, searching for a clue—any clue to who might have sent it.

The card itself was ordinary. The message had been printed in block letters, and there was nothing distinctive about the letters. Nothing, that is, except the color. The warning message had been printed in brown ink.

Justin Dodd's pen had brown ink!

Well, Nancy decided, this certainly looks

incriminating. But as she stared at the card again, she began to wonder just how incriminating it actually was. Would Justin really give himself away like this? Or was someone else trying to frame him?

And if someone was trying to frame Justin, then Nancy was right back at the beginning—with no specific suspect at all.

Nancy set her jaw and straightened her shoulders. Nothing—warnings, poisoned samples, the distrust of the police—nothing was going to keep her from solving this case!

She laid the Spotless sample and the card on a living-room table, then called out, "Hannah, I'm home!" As she opened the door to the kitchen, she added, "Something smells wonderful!"

"It's one of your favorites—beef stew," Hannah Gruen said. "And, yes, you have time to check your phone messages before dinner."

Nancy's eyes widened. "How did you know I was going to ask that?"

Hannah just laughed. "I know you. Besides," she added, "I heard your phone ring a couple of times this afternoon."

"Okay, then. I'll be right back!" Nancy hurried away to replay the messages.

The first was from Bess, who said she was feeling much better.

"Nancy, this is Chief McGinnis," the second message began. "Please call me."

Nancy jotted down the number he gave and called it right away. He's probably not there anymore, she thought.

But the chief was there. "Hello, Nancy," he said in a friendly voice. "Thanks for calling me back. I have just one quick question for you. Did Ned bring me all the samples?"

"That was everything we had left," Nancy replied. "We gave a lot away on Saturday."

"I guess you did. He brought an inventory of what you started out with."

"Any results on the test yet?" Nancy asked.

There was a moment of silence, and Nancy could only guess that the chief was deciding whether or not to tell her. "Well," he admitted at last, "we have done some random checking on the samples Ned brought us."

Quickly Nancy pulled a blank sheet of paper in front of her and got ready to take notes. "Was there poison in any of them?" she asked.

"There was. Your theory was right on the mark. Hang on a second . . . Okay, see you tomorrow," the chief said to someone in the room.

When he returned to the phone, he continued his explanation. "The interesting thing is that not all the samples were tainted. That's why I wondered if there might be more of them. About a quarter of the ones the lab tested were bad. The rest were perfectly all right."

"Were they all from the same batch?" Nancy asked. She knew that manufacturers put code numbers on their products to identify when and where a batch had been made. That way, if they were alerted to a problem, they'd have a way of tracing the individual packages.

"Same batch," Chief McGinnis continued. "The codes looked the same, but we called the manufacturer to be sure. They remembered this group of samples because of its being part of a special project. They also kept part of the batch at the plant," he added. "When they checked it, it was perfectly all right."

"Then maybe it wasn't a problem at the plant," Nancy said. "Maybe it was deliberate tampering."

With a shock, Nancy realized the significance of what she was saying. If Spotless had been tampered with, one of Ned's friends could very easily be the culprit.

"Looks like it," the chief agreed. "I don't see any other answer."

"Did the lab identify the poison?" Nancy went on.

"That was the easy part. When the lab heard that all the victims had had rashes, they had a pretty good idea even without the tests. It was arsenic, Nancy."

Nancy took a deep breath. Arsenic poisoning was a serious crime. Then she realized that something just didn't make sense. Why was Marcia so sick when the other poisoning victims had nothing more than a rash and severe stomach cramps?

"Chief," she asked slowly, "was there the same amount of arsenic in all the poisoned samples?"

"Exactly the same," he said. "Ten milligrams."

Now Nancy really was confused. If all the Spotless samples had the same percentage of arsenic, why was Marcia's reaction so much worse? What piece of the puzzle was Nancy missing?

"One moment, please, and I'll connect you to personnel."

The next morning Nancy was sitting at the desk in her room. She had just read the morning paper. There was a warning printed on the front page not to use any free samples of Spotless. Also the radio and TV had periodic warning announcements. Nancy wondered when the media would find out she was connected with the case. She hoped it wouldn't be too soon, as she had several leads to investigate that day.

Nancy tapped her fingers on the desk while she was put on hold. If she was lucky, she'd soon find out if Justin still worked for Asco.

"I'd like to verify employment," she said when the personnel clerk answered. "The employee's name is Justin Dodd."

"I'm sorry, miss," the clerk said after being gone a moment. "I have no record of a Justin Dodd working for Asco."

Nancy frowned as she hung up. Even though Justin had just been a summer intern, Asco should have had a file on him.

This case is getting stranger by the minute, Nancy thought as she pulled on her coat and left the house.

She headed downtown to one of River Heights's biggest drugstores. Nancy knew Mr. Bailey, the pharmacist, would probably be able to test the sample of Spotless she'd received on her doorstep the day before to see if it contained arsenic.

"What can I do to help you, Nancy?" Mr. Bailey asked when Nancy appeared in his store.

She pulled out the sample of Spotless that she'd found on her front step. "I wondered if you could test this," she said. "I think it might contain arsenic."

Mr. Bailey had obviously read about the case—he wasn't at all surprised. "I'd be glad to help you," he said. "It should only take a few minutes."

When he returned, there was a grim smile on

his face. "You were right," he said. "There's arsenic in it."

"Do you know how much?" Nancy was still puzzled that Marcia's reaction had been so severe. Perhaps, for some reason, there were other samples of Spotless that had more poison in them.

"Ten milligrams," said Mr. Bailey.

The same amount the police had found in the samples they had tested.

"You're working on the Spotless case, right?" asked Mr. Bailey, and Nancy nodded.

Nancy slid the Spotless sample back into her bag. "I just don't understand it. How come some kids have gotten only mildly sick from it, and one girl is in a coma?"

"From the cream?" The pharmacist looked startled. "Someone's in a coma from this cream?"

Nancy nodded.

Mr. Bailey was shaking his head. "That doesn't make sense," he said. "If someone used this cream, they might develop a rash or stomach problems, but they'd never become seriously ill. In order to cause something like a coma, you'd need to swallow the arsenic. A lot of it."

"Are you sure?" Nancy asked.

Mr. Bailey nodded. "I'm telling you, there's just no way this cream could kill you."

Chapter

Twelve

Are you *sure?*" Nancy repeated.

Mr. Bailey looked her straight in the eye.
"There's no doubt in my mind."

"But that means—that means—" Nancy
broke off. It meant Marcia must have ingested
the arsenic. And that meant the case now went
off in about fifty new directions.

"Thank you, Mr. Bailey," Nancy said.
"You've been a big help."

Nancy got back into her car and planned her
next move. First, she wanted to try to see
Marcia. Maybe her condition had stabilized
enough for her to talk. If not, Nancy could
always question one of the doctors. He or she

might be able to tell her something she didn't know about Bess's poisoning.

As she approached the nurses' station on Marcia's floor, Nancy saw she wasn't the only one paying a visit to the hospital that morning. Nancy spotted Heather walking down the hall ahead of her.

"Hi, Heather," she called.

Heather turned and gave her a listless imitation of a smile. "Oh, hi, Nancy," she said. "If you've come to see Marcia, they won't let you in. She's still in a coma. The nurses told me we can call again this afternoon, but she can't have any visitors. Isn't this horrible?"

It certainly was, but at least Heather was treating Nancy like a real person now instead of just someone standing in the way of her getting together with Ned. Nancy wasn't sure what had brought about the change.

Now that I think about it, though, Heather's been acting a lot nicer since we heard about Marcia, Nancy said to herself. She hasn't tried to flirt with Ned once, and she's even being friendly to me.

Looking more closely, Nancy saw Heather's fingers gripping the strap of her shoulder bag as though it were a lifeline. She was clearly nervous about something, and Nancy wondered what it might be.

"I guess there's no point in staying here," Nancy found herself saying. The doctors could wait. "Do you want to stop for a soda or something?"

"Oh, well—well, I guess not," Heather said.

"We can at least walk out to the parking lot together." There, Nancy thought. There's no way Heather can say no to that.

In fact, Heather looked as if she was about to protest again, but then she gave a little shrug and started down the hall. "There's something I just don't understand," Heather commented as they walked toward the hospital's main door.

"What's that?" Nancy asked, watching Heather's eyes for some sign of emotion.

Heather answered slowly, as though she was having trouble voicing her thoughts. "We all used Spotless, but only Bess and Marcia got sick. Why them? Why not me or Brad or Justin or even Ned? Who's singling out Bess and Marcia?"

Nancy shook her head. "I wish I had the answer," she said. She also wished she knew whether Heather's distress was real or fake.

What if Heather was somehow involved in the poisoning and now she wanted a way out? With Marcia in a coma, this case had suddenly become very serious. Maybe it had become too much for Heather. Was that why she and Justin had argued?

As Heather got into her car, Nancy remembered Heather telling Justin that she didn't

want anything to do with it—whatever "it"
was. Could it possibly be more poisonings?

She thought about following Heather but
then remembered she wanted to talk to a
doctor. Instead, Nancy said goodbye to Heather in the parking lot, then turned around and
headed back inside.

"The usual form of arsenic poison is ingest-
ing it—swallowing it," Dr. Perlman, Bess's
doctor, confirmed when he and Nancy were
seated in his cluttered office. "That's why at
first I thought that Bess had eaten something
with poison in it. But it is possible to become
ill from spreading arsenic on the skin."

"And Marcia?" Nancy asked. "Why is she
so sick?"

"Your pharmacist friend is right. The only
explanation is that she must have eaten something that contained arsenic. Lots of arsenic."

"I'm home at last, Hannah," Nancy said as
she sank into one of the comfortable chairs in
the living room. "What a long morning."

The housekeeper came to the doorway.
"How's your case going?" she asked.

Nancy frowned. "Don't ask. I thought I was
close to solving it, and now I feel as though I'm
farther away than ever."

"Maybe you're trying too hard," Hannah
suggested. "Can't you take a day off? You
deserve a break, just like everyone—"

Suddenly Nancy jumped to her feet. "Bess! The concert!" she gasped. "How could I forget?" She turned to Hannah. "How would I survive without you?" she asked affectionately.

"What did I do?" asked a bewildered Hannah.

"Ned and I are going to a concert tonight, and I was supposed to ask Bess," Nancy explained. "I can't believe it—but I forgot all about it." She reached for the phone. "I only hope she hasn't made other plans."

She hadn't.

"Nan, that would be fantastic!" Bess exclaimed when Nancy told her about the Last Night concert. "You know I *love* Last Night."

"And I bet the idea of spending an evening with Brad isn't too painful, either," Nancy teased her.

"I'll make the sacrifice," Bess said with a giggle. "I guess I should start getting ready now."

"Bess, you still have hours!" Nancy protested.

"Just because you can get dressed in twenty minutes doesn't mean I can, Nancy Drew!" Bess said. "Now, I've got to get going. I'll see you tonight."

Nancy had to admit that Bess's primping had paid off. When Nancy, Ned, and Brad arrived at the Marvin house that night, Brad's mouth actually fell open at the sight of Bess.

"You look great," he finally managed to say as Bess slid into the back seat.

Bess did. She had gotten her normal color back, her cold was almost all better, and her rash had all disappeared. And the time she had spent deciding what to wear had definitely been time well spent. Her black leather mini-skirt and blue silk T-shirt looked fantastic, but what was really making Brad stare was Bess's hair. Although the riot of blond curls looked artless, Nancy knew they'd taken hours to arrange.

It was wonderful to see Bess looking so healthy—so much better than healthy, actually. Nancy told her so.

"Well, you look pretty impressive yourself," Ned said with a smile at Nancy's leopard-print minidress with matching stockings. "I think Brad and I are pretty lucky."

"I'm glad you like my outfit." Nancy grinned. "I know it's pretty daring for me. Hey, we'd better get going. I'd hate to miss any of the concert!"

By the time the four of them had gotten to the stadium, they were all cheerful, and even Nancy had pretty much forgotten about the case.

"So tell me about your family . . ." Brad

said to Bess as the four of them settled into their seats.

"It looks as though we don't have to worry about either of them," Nancy said softly to Ned. "They both seem all right tonight."

Ned put his arm around her shoulders. "I'm glad about that. Now you and I can just relax and enjoy the concert." Then he leaned across Nancy to ask Brad, "Do you think they'll sing 'Endless Days'?"

"They'd better. It's my theme song, after all."

"Is that a private joke, or can you share it with us?" asked Bess. She and Nancy both knew the song. Anyone who had ever heard of Last Night knew about their first platinum hit.

"I used to sing it freshman year in college because the term seemed endless," Brad explained. Then he chuckled. "My brother Larry could never relate to it because he works for my dad in our greenhouse. When you're growing plants, endless days are something you want. It's not like college."

Ned laughed. "Nothing's like college."

"That's what I tell my folks," Brad said. "They can't really relate, either. I'm the Chanin trailblazer, the first person in the family to go to college."

"Your parents must be awfully proud," Bess said softly.

"They will be if I do as well as they're hoping," Brad answered.

The lights began to dim. Nancy gave one last look around the hall. "Ned!" she said, grabbing his arm. "Isn't that Justin and Heather over there?"

But before he could find them, the lights were out. A huge roar of cheers went up from the audience—and the concert began.

"The parking lot is going to be a total mess," Ned said when the band had taken its final bow. "Do you guys want to walk around for a few minutes until the crowd thins out?"

"Sounds good to me," Brad agreed, linking his arm with Bess's. "I'm in no hurry to go home."

The park surrounding the stadium was partially wooded. "Let's walk in there," Brad suggested as they came up to it.

"Okay," Ned said, wrapping his arm around Nancy's shoulder. "It's the perfect night for a romantic stroll."

Nancy smiled up at Ned and pecked him on the cheek. "That concert was fantastic. Thanks!"

"I'm glad you liked it," Ned murmured in her ear. "And I'm glad I'm here with you."

Nancy was about to whisper back, when Brad turned around and glanced uneasily over his shoulder. "I don't think anyone's listening," he said. "Remember when I said there was something I needed to tell you guys?"

Nancy nodded. A sudden gust of wind rustled the dry leaves barely clinging to the stately oaks as the moon slid behind a swiftly moving cloud. Bess shivered and inched closer to Brad. "What is it?" she asked in a frightened voice.

Brad lowered his voice to a whisper and motioned the three friends to come together. When they were only a foot apart, he spoke.

"Justin is the poisoner!"

Chapter

Thirteen

BESS GASPED SHARPLY. "*Justin* tried to poison me?" she said.

Nancy realized at that moment that she hadn't told Bess any of her suspicions. It had to be a shock to hear that a friend of Ned's—and Brad's—could be the poisoner.

"I—I just know it's not true. I know it," Bess said rapidly. The harvest moon, free of the trailing clouds, illuminated Bess's face. "He's too nice and funny for that!"

Brad put his hands on her shoulders and looked deep into her eyes. "You never know everything about people," he said earnestly.

"But don't worry—you're safe now. No one's going to hurt you anymore."

"Why do you think Justin is the poisoner?" Nancy asked. She kept her voice as neutral as possible. Brad had voiced her own suspicion, but she didn't want to lead him in any way. He doesn't know what I know about Justin, she reminded herself. But what *does* he know?

Once again Brad glanced nervously over his shoulder. The crackle of brittle leaves sounded as if someone was advancing toward the little group.

"It just makes sense," he said in a low voice. "He worked for Asco, and they're ruthless. They have the best reason for wanting Spotless to fail. Plus Justin's very loyal—too loyal. I'm sure it's got to be him."

A loud thud interrupted Brad before he could go on. Everyone jumped, and Bess gave a smothered shriek. "What was that?" she whispered.

Ned looked around for a second—then chuckled. He bent down and picked up a big pine cone. "Here's the villain," he said, tossing it aside.

Brad blew out a breath and went on. "The way I figure it, Asco must have paid Justin to tamper with the samples. It would have been so easy for him. Remember, he used to be a chemistry major."

"That's right!" Bess exclaimed. "I'd forgotten that!" She looked at Brad with dots of moonlight dancing in her eyes. "You've got to be right. Everything points to Justin, doesn't it?"

She turned excitedly to Nancy. "You're going to talk to Chief McGinnis about him, aren't you? With Marcia still so sick, he's got to know!"

Nancy nodded slowly. Brad's reasoning was exactly like her own. She'd been looking for someone with both opportunity and motive. Justin had the opportunity—and Asco had the motive. It did all fit.

Except that there was no evidence.

If I'd been able to find Justin's personnel file, Nancy thought, I would have known for sure if he's being paid by Asco. But until I can confirm his employment, I have no concrete proof.

Besides, there was a flaw in the theory—a flaw Brad didn't know about. Even if Justin had poisoned the Spotless samples, he might not be the person who had poisoned Marcia. It was entirely possible the two poisonings were unconnected.

Nancy didn't say any of this aloud. "I'll call the chief tomorrow," Nancy told Bess.

Bess looked relieved. "Then can I ask everyone a favor?" she asked. "Could we drop the subject of these poisonings for the rest of the evening?"

"I heartily second the motion," said Ned, and Nancy and Brad both nodded their agreement.

"Okay. Subject is officially changed," said Bess. "I'm changing it to Brad. Did you know his father has a greenhouse?"

Nancy grinned. This was a total change of subject. "I heard him mention that, yes," she said.

"Well," Bess went on, "don't you think we should get some Halloween pumpkins there?"

"Bess, we haven't carved pumpkins in about ten—"

"I was just telling Brad how much we always look forward to making our jack-o'-lanterns," Bess went on meaningfully. "And he said we're all welcome to come out to the greenhouse and pick some out."

"I think that would be great," Nancy said hastily. She'd suddenly gotten the message. It wasn't the pumpkins Bess cared about—it was seeing Brad again. "If your father has a good supply, tell him to save us a bunch," she told Brad.

"Oh, he's got tons," said Brad. "I'll give you directions to the greenhouse before we go home tonight—you can all come over sometime tomorrow." The smile he flashed at Bess told Nancy he was looking forward to the next day as much as Bess was.

The four of them had started walking along

the narrow path again. Nancy held Ned's hand tightly. The woods were deliciously spooky— just right for Halloween.

"Do you think Justin's still going to have his party?" Brad asked over his shoulder. He and Bess were walking ahead of Nancy and Ned.

"Why wouldn't he?" asked Ned.

"Well—um—" It was clear that Brad was uncomfortable. Then Nancy understood why.

"We don't know for certain that he was the one who poisoned the samples," she reminded him. She definitely wanted to go to the party— it would be a great chance to watch Justin more closely.

Bess turned to Brad. "Are you going?"

Brad smiled down into her eyes. "I wouldn't miss a party with you, Bess." Brad linked his arm through Bess's, and they quickened their pace to put some distance between them and Nancy and Ned.

"I guess he wants a little privacy," said Nancy with a laugh.

"I'm not complaining," Ned answered. "I wanted some time alone with my girl, too." Ned put his arm around Nancy's shoulder and drew her close.

They slowed their steps and finally stopped in the hazy pool of light cast down by a lamp post at the edge of the woods. Ned put his hands on Nancy's shoulders, slowly drew her close, and gently pressed his lips to hers. "Do you know how long I've been wanting to do that?" he murmured into her ear. "But I guess we can't stay here," he continued reluctantly. "We'd better find the others."

"Before we do, I need your advice," said Nancy.

"Sure! Professor Nickerson to the rescue."

Briefly Nancy outlined what she had learned from Dr. Perlman and Mr. Bailey. "Doesn't it sound to you as though we have two poisoners on our hands?" she finished.

Ned looked very grim. "It sure does. I just wish we could talk to Marcia and ask her what she ate or drank," he said, his voice full of frustration.

"I know. This case is so confusing. Just when I think I've solved it, something happens and my theory falls apart!"

"You'll figure it out. I have absolute faith in you," said Ned softly. He pulled Nancy to him and kissed her again.

They broke away when they heard someone talking very nearby. It didn't sound like Bess or Brad.

"Is that Heather?" Nancy asked in surprise.

She and Ned looked around, but there was no sign of anyone else. "This way!" Nancy whispered, and they walked quickly up the path to the spot where they'd heard the voices. But there was no one there.

"I wonder if it could be Heather and Justin,"

Nancy said. "I really did think I saw them just after the show."

"It's strange to think they'd be anywhere together, though," Ned pointed out. "I mean, after the way they were fighting yesterday—"

There was a rustling in the bushes ahead of them. "Bess?" Nancy called softly.

No answer.

"I didn't hear anything," said Ned.

The two of them started walking again—and the sound resumed. This time Ned squeezed Nancy's hand to show her that he'd heard it, too.

The two of them slowed their pace. Whatever was moving through the dry leaves slowed down, too.

They walked more quickly. As if it were an echo, the rustling noise sped up.

They stopped. And an instant later, the sound stopped.

When Nancy looked at Ned, he nodded.

There was no doubt about it. Someone was following them!

Chapter
Fourteen

W HO'S THERE?" Nancy called sharply.

Dead silence—and then whoever had been following them began to run. This time, there was no attempt to be quiet. Crashing, stumbling, trampling through the underbrush, the invisible follower raced to get away.

"You take the path. I'll take the woods!" Nancy said, and she dashed off into the trees in pursuit.

Branches whipped across her face, and the undergrowth tangled around her ankles. The ground was treacherously uneven and littered with fallen branches. Nancy tripped over one and fell full-length to the ground. Gasping for breath, she yanked herself to her feet and ran on, but the delay had cost her precious seconds. Ahead of her, the noises faded and disappeared.

Whoever had been following them was gone.

Slowly Nancy retraced her steps to the path. Ned was just returning to the spot where they'd separated. "I lost him," he said heavily.

"Me, too. Did you see anything?"

"Not a glimpse. He must have known these woods, because he just disappeared."

"I didn't see anything, either," said Nancy with a sigh. "And the only noise I heard was him getting farther and farther away."

She rubbed her face, which was stinging from the branches that had scratched it. "Well, we got some exercise, anyway," she said ruefully.

"I think I'll try the gym next time," Ned quipped. "It's less stressful." He glanced at his watch. "We're late," he said. "Brad and Bess will be waiting for us."

"I don't imagine they'll complain about a little more time alone, do you?" asked Nancy with a grin.

"Probably not. Still, let's find them and ask if they saw who was chasing us."

Neither Brad nor Bess had noticed anything. In any case, they were having such a good time together that it was impossible to get a serious word out of either one.

"Nancy, this girl is being deliberately cruel," Brad said when the four of them were back in the car.

"What's the problem?" Nancy asked.

"She's refusing to tell me what costume she's wearing to the party," Brad said in a hurt voice. "Don't you think she should trust me more than that?"

They had stopped at a traffic light, and Ned turned toward the back seat. "Would you believe that Bess is going to be Jane and I'm going to be Tarzan?" he asked.

"You'd better not be! Nancy's your girl, remember?"

Bess laughed. "I guess you'll have to come to the party to see if you can recognize me. I'm not sure what I'll be. George called and said she went to Chicago today to pick out our costumes. She was very mysterious about her choices. I just hope I don't turn out to be the back end of a horse."

"Don't worry, Bess," said Brad. "Even if you are, I'll recognize you."

The jokes and teasing kept up until Ned had dropped off Brad and Bess. But the instant Bess waved goodbye, Ned turned to Nancy.

"Can we go back to the case for a second? There's one thing I don't understand," he said.

The headlights of an oncoming car played on his face at that moment, and Nancy could see that his forehead was furrowed in thought.

"I just can't buy Asco being involved in the poisoning," he said finally.

"That's been bothering me, too!" Nancy burst out. "I know industrial espionage happens," she added. "But I can't believe that any major company would try poisoning."

"That's exactly what I'm having trouble with," Ned agreed. "Also, it seems to me that if people are afraid to use Spotless, they'd think twice before buying *any* skin cream. If that happened, Clearly would suffer almost as much as Spotless.

"You know," Ned mused, "I think I'll call my marketing professor tomorrow morning. He knows a lot about both Asco and Spotless. He may be able to help us."

"That's a great idea, Ned. We could really use some perspective on this thing."

"I got the costumes!" George sang out as she walked through the front door of the Drew house the next afternoon.

At the sound of her voice, Nancy and Bess ran downstairs.

"Let's see them! Let's see them!" Bess said excitedly. She pounced on the four boxes that George was trying to balance, and they all slid to the ground. Bess grabbed the top one. "Is this mine?"

"Bess, let George pass them out," Nancy protested.

"But I want to see my costume!" Bess wailed.

"It is the one in the box you're holding," George said. "And I hope you like it."

Bess yanked the box open and rummaged eagerly through the folds of pink tissue inside. "Dorothy!" she squealed. "George, that's perfect! *The Wizard of Oz* is still one of my favorite movies, you know!"

"I know," said George with a grin. "And you're perfect for Dorothy."

She smiled wickedly at Nancy. "You're the Scarecrow. Hope you don't mind. I'm the Tin Man, and Ned is the Cowardly Lion."

Nancy burst out laughing. "I'll let *you* tell him that. He'll certainly look cute, though!"

She picked up the box with her own costume and tried on the raggedy straw hat inside. "How's it look?" she asked.

"Perfect," said George. "Not a brain in your head. And speaking of no brains, guess who I saw in Chicago?"

"No idea."

George unzipped her jacket and tossed it over the couch. "Try Heather Tompkins."

Nancy stared at her in astonishment. "Did you talk to her? What was she doing there?"

"I don't think she saw me," George answered. "Which is probably lucky, as far as she's concerned. I doubt she'd have wanted to know I saw her."

"Why? Where did you see her?" asked Bess.

"Coming out of the Premier Advertising Agency."

"Isn't that the ad agency for Spotless?" asked Bess.

"Yup," George said.

"But Heather told me she's dropping out of the marketing program," Nancy said blankly. "Why would she be talking to the people at Premier? It's got to have something to do with the marketing program, but—"

"Nancy, this is very interesting, but can we think about it on the way to Brad's?" Bess interrupted.

Nancy gave her a puzzled stare. "To Brad's?" she repeated.

"It's almost three o'clock," Bess said patiently. "I told Brad we'd get to his father's greenhouse at three. Pumpkins—remember?"

Nancy stifled a groan. She'd completely forgotten about the pumpkin-gathering expedition. Visiting a greenhouse was the last thing she felt like doing, but she had promised Bess.

"Want to come with us to buy pumpkins?" she asked George, grabbing the keys to the Mustang. "Not that Bess is really interested in the pumpkins—"

"I'd love to come," said George. "It'll be nice to have a ride in the country."

The three girls made their way out of River Heights and into the surrounding countryside. After a short drive, they spotted a sign for Chanin's Nursery.

The Chanin family's greenhouses were set back from the road, but a fruit stand next to the driveway beckoned the girls with a colorful array of bright red apples, brilliant gourds and Indian corn, and baskets of grapes.

"I'm hungry," Bess said as Nancy parked the car. "Let's make sure we get a few apples, at least. And maybe some cider, and let's see if they have any maple syrup—"

"Can I help you, girls?"

Nancy, Bess, and George turned to see a tall man in a gray sweater, faded jeans, and heavy work boots walking toward them. His once-blond hair was mostly gray now, but there was no mistaking his resemblance to Brad.

"Oh, hi," said Bess nervously. "We were looking for Brad. I mean, for pumpkins! I mean—"

"You must be Bess," the man said, his eyes twinkling. "I'm Ted Chanin, Brad's father. Brad said you might come this afternoon. I asked him to make a delivery, but I expect him back soon. Can I show you anything in the meantime?"

"Well, as Bess said, we're interested in pumpkins," Nancy told him.

"Then you came to the right place."

Mr. Chanin led them down a little path between two greenhouses. "Just a minute," he said, pulling open a creaky old door to step into a small gardening shed. When he came out, he was pushing a wheelbarrow.

"The pumpkin patch is back here," he said, once again leading the way. "More than half of them have been sold already, though."

George gasped. "This is incredible!" she said as they walked behind the second green-house. There, in the field behind it, were rows and rows and rows of huge pumpkins.

"I've never seen such enormous pumpkins," Nancy said to Mr. Chanin as Bess and George began walking through the field. "What's your secret?"

Mr. Chanin shook his head. "No secret. Just hard work. We get lots of full sun here, of course. The soil's well drained, and we use a lot of fertilizer. And, of course, we do use a couple of pesticides, though we don't advertise that fact . . ."

Nancy was itching to join her friends, but Brad's father kept on talking. Now he was pointing to the rows with the largest pumpkins.

"Take those," he said. "That strain was

susceptible to vine borer this year, so we had to use a stronger insecticide than normal."

Nancy gave the pumpkins an admiring glance. "It must have worked," she said politely.

Mr. Chanin grinned. "Arsenic does it—every time."

Chapter
Fifteen

A RSENIC!

Nancy stared at Mr. Chanin for a long moment, her mind whirling. For a second she actually felt faint.

Has the answer been here all the time? she thought. Is this greenhouse the source of—

"Mr. Chanin, there's a customer here who says she has to talk to you right away." Nancy and Brad's father turned to see a harried-looking employee. "It's that woman who's always calling us to complain. She claims you deliberately sold her a bushel of bruised apples, and she wants her money back."

"Oh, dear," said Mr. Chanin mildly. "Yes, I

know the woman you're talking about. Could you tell her I'll be right there? Please excuse me," he said to Nancy. "I'd better go straighten this out. Nice talking to you."

He waved and disappeared into the greenhouse before Nancy had a chance to ask him anything else.

"Hey, Nan! Are you going to help us, or what?" George hollered from the middle of the pumpkin field.

"Here I come!" Nancy called back as she slowly began walking toward her friends. She was still reeling from what Mr. Chanin had told her.

Before she'd reached Bess and George, though, Nancy heard footsteps thudding in the dirt behind her. She turned and saw Brad racing toward them.

"Sorry I'm late," he panted as he caught up to them. He smiled at Nancy and George, but his brightest smile was for Bess.

"No problem," George told him. "Bess and I have done a wonderful job picking pumpkins out all by ourselves. Or maybe I should say Bess has. She wants about five hundred of them. It's a good thing your dad brought us a wheelbarrow."

"But I still can't decide between these two," Bess said plaintively, pointing to two massive pumpkins. "They're both great."

"Why don't you take them both?" Nancy

suggested absentmindedly. Her thoughts were still on what Brad's father had told her.

Brad spoke up. "I agree with Nancy. Take them both."

"You're a great salesman," said Bess with a giggle. "Do you need any help pushing the wheelbarrow?"

"I just need your company," said Brad cheerfully as he hoisted the second of the gigantic pumpkins into the wheelbarrow and trundled it down to the parking lot.

George and Nancy followed more slowly. When they reached the parking lot, Bess called out, "Nancy, we've just about filled the trunk of your car!"

"There's room for two more in the back—as long as they're not those fifty-pound monsters Bess seems to like," Brad said.

"Come help me pick the best two," Bess called to George, and they raced back to the field.

When the two girls were out of earshot, Brad breathed a sigh of relief and turned to Nancy.

"I was hoping I'd get a chance to talk to you alone," he said. Brad's expression was deadly serious, and he was speaking so quietly Nancy could hardly hear him. This time, though, she found his manner odd. Why was Brad always acting so secretive?

"What is it?" Nancy asked.

"I wanted to talk to you about Justin," Brad

127

replied. "I know you're a detective, so you've faced these problems before. What do we do first—call the police or call Emerson?"

His question took Nancy by surprise. "Why would we call the college?" she asked. "Even if Justin is the poisoner, there's no reason for us to call his school."

Brad gave her a look that said the answer to that was obvious. "Justin should be expelled for what he did!" he said incredulously.

"Well, maybe so," said Nancy. "But I'm still puzzled about one thing, Brad." She was telling the truth. "I can understand why Justin might tamper with the samples to help Asco, but why would he want to hurt Marcia, too?"

Brad took off his glasses and polished them on his handkerchief. "I don't think Justin hurt Marcia deliberately," he said slowly. "But Marcia was always worried about her skin. She must have used too much Spotless—that's why she's so much worse off than the other patients."

It was a good theory except for one thing. No matter how much Spotless Marcia had slathered on her face, it wouldn't have caused a coma. Whatever the source of Marcia's arsenic had been, it wasn't Spotless.

Nancy didn't mention that to Brad, of course. Instead she just said, "I think the best thing to do is to wait until the party. Justin may give us a clue then." And I'm still not convinced Justin's the one, she added to herself, giving Brad a searching look.

"Okay," Brad said, avoiding Nancy's eyes. "I guess we'll figure out a way to turn him in after that. I just hope he doesn't try anything else in the meantime."

"Hi, Ned, it's me," Nancy said. "Did you talk to your professor?"

She had just come home from dropping off Bess, George, and about three hundred pounds of pumpkins. She had said a quick hello to Hannah and dashed up to her telephone.

Ned's answer was about what Nancy had expected. "The professor confirmed what we'd already been thinking. Asco would lose more than it would gain by poisoning Spotless. Remember what happened after the sleeping pill scare? Sales of all sleeping pills dropped. Professor Martin doesn't think Asco would risk anything like that."

Nancy stared out the window, watching the leaves fall off the trees. Even without knowing much about marketing, she felt sure Ned's professor was right.

"Professor Martin also said that he knows the president of Asco personally," Ned continued. "He says he'd never let his company be involved in sabotage—he's much too principled for that."

"Thanks, Ned," Nancy said gratefully.

"Things are starting to come together for me at last."

As she hung up the phone, Nancy pulled a pad and pencil from her desk and began to doodle. She drew a row of squares and connected them to a row of triangles. Then she started to color in half of each square. And all the time that her hand was busy drawing, her mind was busy putting things together.

The pieces were starting to fit.

It all hinged on the basics: motive and opportunity.

Justin had the opportunity and the specialized knowledge to poison the samples. But what was his motive?

It seemed almost certain that he wasn't being paid by Asco, despite what Brad had said. And if Asco wasn't paying Justin to tamper with the Spotless samples, what reason did he have for poisoning them? None that Nancy could find.

She and Ned had focused on Justin's chemistry background. But there was someone else —someone who had done even better in chemistry than Justin. Someone who had easy access to arsenic.

Nancy thought back. Justin had been the obvious suspect, but what if someone had tried to frame him?

Each time it had been suggested that Justin was the poisoner, Brad had been the one to make the suggestion. And who kept reminding Nancy of Justin's chemistry background? Brad. He'd also been the person who'd first brought up Justin's job with Asco and who had suggested the link between Asco and the poisoned samples.

It could also have been Brad who used a brown pen to write the threatening note when he left that poisoned sample of Spotless on Nancy's front porch. He could hardly have missed the fact that Justin always wrote with brown ink.

It was starting to look as though Brad had been lying.

The question was why. Why did Brad want everyone to think Justin was the poisoner?

Nancy thought back to Brad's comments that afternoon. At the time she had thought it was strange that he wanted to tell Emerson as well as the police about Justin's guilt. Surely that was a story for the police, not a college.

"Justin should be expelled for what he did!" Brad had said. Was that his goal—getting Justin expelled? According to Ned, Brad and Justin were the top students in the marketing program. It was likely one of them would get the job in Chicago. Was the poisoning an elaborate way to be sure that Brad was the winner?

"But even if that's true, why would Brad want to hurt Marcia?" Nancy asked aloud.

Marcia wasn't a serious contender for the job with Premier. Was her poisoning connected to the Spotless samples—or could there be two poisoners?

With a grim smile, Nancy rose to her feet.

There *may* be two, she thought. But I know for sure that there's at least one. And now I know who he is.

Chapter
Sixteen

"THIS IS TERRIFIC!" Bess said as she surveyed her friends' costumes.

"What I like are the props. They're what really make these costumes. I can't believe they gave us Toto, too!"

George, whose Tin Man costume fit her just right, held out her oil can and gestured at the stuffed dog Bess was holding. With her blond hair hidden under a dark wig, Toto snuggled in her arms, and ruby slippers on her feet, Bess made a perfect Dorothy.

Ned put his arm around Nancy's shoulders and gave her a big lion's-paw hug. "No one would ever recognize you in that Scarecrow costume," he said.

"Actually, I'm counting on at least one person at the party to recognize me."

Nancy's face was very serious. "Bess, George, I've already told Ned this. I think I've figured out who poisoned the Spotless samples. I wanted you to know before we got to the party."

Bess was putting on her makeup in the mirror. "But we already know, Nan. It was Justin."

Nancy paused.

"Wasn't it?" asked Bess.

"I don't think so," Nancy said.

"But Bess told me all the evidence pointed to him," said George.

"It does, but that's only because he was being framed," Nancy explained.

"What do you mean? Who framed him?" asked George. "Heather? Is that why she was in Chicago?"

Nancy shook her head.

"But, Nancy, there's only one person left besides Marcia," Bess said uneasily. "I know you're not trying to say that—"

Nancy rose and put her hand on Bess's shoulder. "Yes, I am," she said sympathetically. "I hate to tell you this, Bess, but it looks like Brad's the poisoner."

For a second Bess just stared at her. Then

she gave a wavering little smile. "No, that's not possible," she said. "I know Brad. He's—he's just not that kind of person."

"I'm afraid he is, Bess," said Ned quietly. "It was a shock to me, too. He's fooled us all."

"But why?" George asked, astonished.

Nancy explained. "He wanted to discredit Justin so he'd get the job at the ad agency. It's as simple as that."

"Brad wants that job badly," Ned put in. "I agree with Nancy. He'll do anything to get it."

"Even making Marcia so sick? And—and me?" Bess's voice was filled with horror.

"He's a very good actor," Nancy said. "But I'm sure he wasn't pretending with you, Bess. I think he really likes you."

Bess shuddered. "I don't know whether that's good or bad!" she wailed.

"I don't, either," said Nancy. "Bess, please don't leave the party alone with him for any reason. I'm planning to confront him there, and I don't trust what he's going to do."

"I won't even talk to him," Bess vowed.

This time it was Ned who shook his head. "That won't work, either. Let Nancy handle it, but until she does, you both need to pretend nothing has happened."

"But he's a poisoner!" Bess protested.

George turned to her cousin. "Well, then, this is your chance to prove you're as good at acting as he is."

"Bess, this is very important," Nancy said softly.

"Okay, I'll do it," said Bess. Her chin was trembling, but there was a look of dogged determination in her eye. "You guys are about to see an Academy Award–winning performance."

Even if she hadn't been there earlier that day to drop off the pumpkins, Nancy would have had no trouble finding Justin's house. Cars lined the street, and the sound of rock music drifted out to meet the four friends as they pulled up beside the curb.

"Hi, everybody!" Justin called as they entered the house. "Your costumes are great!"

"So is yours," George replied cheerfully. Justin was dressed as a mad scientist. With his rumpled lab coat and his curly hair standing on end, he looked the part perfectly.

To the right of the foyer was the living room, filled with people in brightly colored costumes. Nancy's eyes scanned the group. "Have Brad and Heather gotten here yet?" she asked Justin.

"Not yet. Heather said she might be a little late. Help yourself to punch!" Justin pointed to the dining room on their left, where a long table was crammed with food. A huge ceramic pumpkin in the middle of the table held punch.

"Well, I'd like to work up an appetite before I eat," said Ned. "Want to dance, Nancy?"

He took her by the arm and led her into Justin's huge living room, where all the furniture had been pushed against the walls. "This gives us a chance to talk," he said as he pulled her close, "and you can watch for Brad."

At that moment the front door opened again, and Heather floated into the foyer, wearing a picture-perfect Cinderella costume. "She looks great," Nancy said. "Still no Brad, though. I wonder where he is."

"He'll be here." Ned sounded confident. "He doesn't know we suspect him, remember. Didn't you tell him you were going to confront Justin?" Ned pulled her closer and spoke into her ear. No one watching them would have known they were discussing a case. "Being Brad, he won't want to miss that. That's what he's been working toward—having Justin discredited."

Over Ned's shoulder, Nancy caught a glimpse of Bess dancing with Justin. Her friend was smiling as though she didn't have a care in the world. Good for you, Bess! Nancy thought. You're on your way to Hollywood!

"Excuse me, Nickerson, but this is my dance."

Nancy kept a smile on her face as the hooded monk tapped Ned's shoulder. With his hood drawn low over his face, it was hard to distinguish his features—but Nancy recognized his voice immediately.

"Hello, Brad," she said as Ned moved away. "I didn't see you come in. What movie are you from?"

"Oh, I didn't bother with that," Brad said.

From this angle Nancy could see his face, and what she saw disturbed her. Had Brad's eyes always looked that cold, or did they only seem that way now that she knew the truth about him?

"I need to talk to you, Nancy," he said. For some reason, Brad was nervous. But why?

He took her hand and led her toward the patio. "Can we talk out there?" he asked.

"But, Brad, it's freezing out there!" Nancy protested in what she hoped was a merry voice.

"We'll need some privacy," Brad answered shortly.

Though Nancy nodded, she was uneasy. She didn't want to confront Brad in the crowded room, but she was reluctant to be alone with him. As she followed Brad out of the room, she caught Ned's eye and tossed her head slightly in the direction of the patio. She hoped he'd recognize the signal she was sending him.

The instant the two of them were out on the patio, Brad asked, "Why aren't the police here yet? I thought we agreed you'd call them and have them arrest Justin at the party."

Nancy took a deep breath. The time to confront Brad had arrived.

"I didn't call them," she said in a quiet voice. "They have no reason to arrest an innocent person. You and I both know that Justin didn't poison those Spotless samples."

"What are you talking about?" Brad demanded harshly. "Of course he did!"

Nancy shook her head slowly. "It won't work anymore, Brad." She heard him gasp sharply and knew her words had hit home.

"What—what are you talking about?" he blustered.

"I know now that you're the one who put the arsenic in the jars of Spotless," Nancy continued. "I even know where you got the poison. Your father told me all about the arsenic he uses on his plants."

There was a moment of silence. Was Brad trying to invent another excuse?

"That's a crazy thing to say," Brad told her calmly. He moved forward and grabbed both her shoulders. His hood had fallen back, and Nancy could see that his face was contorted with rage. But his voice was calm when he spoke again.

"I'd never poison anyone. You obviously think you're a great detective, Nancy. But where's your evidence?"

"Where's yours?" Nancy countered. "Asco had nothing to do with these poisonings, and neither did Justin. So why did you keep telling me they did?"

Brad just stared at her. Then, with a swift motion, he flung Nancy down and raced off.

For a moment Nancy lay there stunned, but she quickly scrambled to her feet. She had to catch him!

Brad had the advantage of a head start. By the time Nancy reached the front of the house, he was already in his car revving the engine.

Nancy slid behind the wheel of the Mustang and fumbled under the seat for the extra key. "I'm not going to let you get away, Brad," she muttered under her breath. Her hand found the key.

Nancy turned on the ignition, and the Mustang burst to life with a roar.

Brad's car screeched around the near corner, careening dangerously. Nancy followed at a safe distance. The important thing was to keep him in sight. Once he stopped, she'd confront him.

But he didn't stop. Within a few minutes they were outside the city limits. Were they driving to Brad's father's greenhouses?

The Chanin greenhouses were silhouetted in yellow light from the moon when Nancy pulled into the parking lot. Brad's car was already there, but it was empty. Where was he?

Slowly Nancy walked between the two large greenhouses, alert for any sound. Was Brad in one of the buildings? He couldn't have gotten far.

As Nancy tiptoed toward the second greenhouse, there was a faint creaking sound.

It was the same sound she had heard that afternoon when Mr. Chanin had brought the wheelbarrow out of the gardening shed. Now she knew where Brad was.

Cautiously Nancy made her way to the shed. She tipped her head to one side, listening for Brad. He was inside the shed—she was sure of it.

Nancy reached for the door handle and pulled it slowly. The creaking she'd heard before sounded again.

"I know you're in there, Brad," Nancy said steadily as she moved into the gardening shed.

Nothing but silence greeted her—until Nancy heard the rush of air beside her ear. The sound intensified before the blow connected. Then the whole world went quiet and black.

Chapter

Seventeen

GRADUALLY THE DARKNESS lightened. Nancy moved slightly—and moaned. Her head was throbbing, and she had no idea where she was. Slowly she opened her eyes to slits.

The first thing she saw was Brad Chanin's smile—a smile so full of malice that it took Nancy's breath away.

"So you decided to wake up," he said with a nasty chuckle. "That's nice. Now you can hear what I've planned for Nancy Drew, famous girl detective."

The haze was clearing from her head now. We're in the gardening shed, Nancy thought. That much I remember.

Looking down, she saw that she was propped up in a chair. Brad must have dragged her there—before he bound her wrists and ankles in front of her.

"What is it you've planned?" Nancy asked. Though her heart was pounding, she forced her voice to stay calm. The longer she could keep Brad talking, the better her chances of getting away.

Nancy realized with relief that Brad had turned on the overhead light. The darkness would have been to his advantage, since Nancy was unfamiliar with the inside of the shed. But now she could see—and her eyes were searching for anything that would help her get out.

Brad was between Nancy and the door. She'd have to distract him.

But what was he doing now?

Flashing her another evil smile, he picked up a hose with a funnel-shaped nozzle from the floor. He fitted the hose onto a large metal cylinder and walked slowly toward her, dragging the cylinder behind him.

"You're going to die, Nancy Drew," he said with a smile.

Nancy forced herself to remain calm. Brad had made mistakes before. If she could trick him into another one, she'd have a chance. "You'll never get away with this," she said in a reasonable voice.

"Oh, yes, I will, and everyone will think it was an accident."

Nancy raised one eyebrow. "An accident when my hands and feet are tied? The police will never believe that!"

"Oh, they will when I get done." Brad gestured toward the cylinder. "This is a fogger, the kind we use to kill pests on roses. It kills other pests, too." He chuckled, obviously amused by his own wit.

"First, I'm going to give you just enough to make you unconscious. Then I'll wait until you're out and give you the rest. When the police arrive, it'll be too late. River Heights's prize snoop will be gone."

Stall, Nancy told herself. The longer you can keep him talking, the better.

"You've thought this all out, haven't you?" she asked, trying to make her voice sound admiring. "Why did you poison the Spotless samples in the first place?"

"Easy." Brad opened one of the drawers on the workbench and pulled out a gas mask. "I had to do something to get Justin out of the marketing program. If he was suspected of sabotaging the samples, Emerson would expel him. Then he'd be sure not to get that job at Premier."

"Is the job that important to you?"

The light glinted off Brad's glasses. "I've got to be the best—understand? Heather wasn't much competition, but Justin just wouldn't give up." He shook his head in disbelief.

"Very clever," Nancy said dryly. "But I still don't understand why you poisoned Marcia."

Brad started to slip the gas mask over his face, then paused. "Marcia was too nosy for her own good. We went out for a while. Did you know that?" He smiled smugly. "She broke up with me because she said I was obsessed with getting ahead. Can you imagine breaking up with someone because he was too ambitious?

"She wouldn't stop nagging me," he went on. "She saw the arsenic in my car the night we were all at Heather's—and she threatened to tell everyone I was poisoning the samples."

So that was the explanation for Marcia's phone call.

"I would have been expelled for that," Brad continued. "So naturally I couldn't let her get away with it. I followed her home that day at lunch. It was so easy."

There was no mistaking the gloat in his voice.

"I told her I had stolen the questionnaires. When she went out to check on them, I just slipped a little arsenic into her soda."

"But you miscalculated," Nancy said. "She didn't die."

Brad stared at her. "I never meant to kill Marcia! All I wanted to do was make her sick enough so that she'd know I was serious. Then she'd keep her mouth shut!"

For the first time his words gave Nancy a glimmer of hope. "You don't really want to kill me, either, then?" she asked.

"No, I don't." Brad frowned. "All I want is that job at Premier. But you're not as easy to scare as Marcia," he said crossly. "I tried to frighten you with the poisoned sample and the threatening note. Those didn't work." He pulled the cylinder closer. "I kept telling you that Justin was the poisoner, but you refused to believe me. Sorry, Nancy," he said sadly. "I have no choice. You've got to die."

He reached for the gas mask again. It was now or never.

Nancy flung herself forward. Using her head as a battering ram, she crashed into Brad and knocked him to the ground. She heard a groan —and then there was silence.

He's only stunned, Nancy reminded herself, but it will give me a few seconds to get out of the shed.

Struggling desperately against the wire that bound her feet and hands, Nancy tried to stand. It was no use. Until she could free her feet, she wouldn't be able to get off the floor.

How far am I from the workbench? She thought frantically. There has to be some kind of knife or clippers there.

Nancy rolled over and over, wincing in agony as the wires cut into her wrists and ankles.

One more turn, and I'll be there!

Then she'd reached it. Nancy rolled onto her side and raised herself up on her elbow. With painful slowness she worked the bottom drawer open and felt feverishly inside it.

A roll of plant wire. A trowel. A gardening fork. The clippers. Nancy pulled them out with the tips of her fingers.

"Oh, no, you don't!" Brad loomed over her now.

He grabbed her by the shoulder and yanked her away from the workbench. As he did, the clippers flew out of her hands.

"You're not getting away!" Brad yelled furiously. "That job is mine. You can't stop me!"

Brad had to bend down to pull Nancy away from the workbench—and that was his undoing.

Nancy brought her knees to her chest, kicked out with all her might—and sent Brad sprawling.

Before he could rise to his feet again, she clasped her bound hands together and slammed them into his throat.

Then, at last, she knew he'd be no more trouble.

Gasping with relief, Nancy began to lurch

toward the clippers again. At that moment she heard Ned's voice.

"Nancy! Nancy! Where are you?"

She heard footsteps racing across the gravel toward the lighted shed—and in a moment Ned was kneeling at her side.

"Are you okay?" he gasped.

Nancy nodded and smiled shakily. "I'll feel better when Brad's in police custody, though. And when I can walk again."

She gestured to the clippers, which had landed on the other side of the shed. Ned grabbed them and cut the wires around her feet and hands.

"Better tie Brad up," Nancy said as she rubbed her wrists to get the circulation back.

Ned obliged, rolling Brad's limp form over to tie his hands behind him.

Then he drew Nancy into his arms. "I was so worried," he said huskily. "I had no idea where he'd taken you! I tried his house, but he wasn't there. If I hadn't gotten here in time—"

"But you did." Nancy kissed him. Then she looked down at his costume and grinned. "I was never so glad to see a cowardly lion."

After Nancy and Ned had answered Chief McGinnis's questions, and Brad was safely locked up, they drove back to Justin's house. The party had broken up long ago—but

Heather, Justin, Bess, and George were still there, waiting anxiously.

Bess hurled herself at Nancy. "Where were you?" she cried. "We were so worried! And what happened to you? You look awful!"

Nancy glanced down at herself. The Scarecrow costume was definitely looking more raggedy than it had when it came out of the box.

"We wanted to help," George chimed in, "but we didn't know where you'd gone. You and Ned just disappeared!"

"Well, we've been all over the place," Nancy said. She told them all what had happened to her in the past few hours.

When she had finished, Justin's face was white. "I was afraid of something like this," he said. "But I just couldn't make myself believe Brad would do something so horrible to Marcia!"

"What made you think Brad was lying?" Ned asked him.

"Remember how the police asked each of us where we were when Marcia was poisoned?" Justin said. "Brad claimed he'd been shopping in the mall, but I knew he hadn't been. When I came back to the mall after I left you two at the Mexican restaurant, I saw Brad's car pulling into the parking lot. I knew he'd gone somewhere."

"But why didn't you tell us?" Nancy asked.

Justin's expression was a little sheepish. "It looked like everyone already suspected me. You knew I'd worked for Asco—and you all seemed to think that was some kind of crime. I figured no one would believe me unless some-one else could back me up. They'd think I was just trying to shift the blame."

She smiled ruefully at Justin. "I did suspect you," she said. "I tried to find out whether you were still working for Asco, but your personnel files had disappeared. That seemed awfully suspicious—like some kind of cover-up."

Justin looked puzzled. "Asco's got my file. They called me today to ask if I wanted to work during semester break."

"Well, that's another mystery solved," Nancy said lightly. "The file wasn't hidden. It was just sitting on someone's desk!"

There was only one more question. Nancy looked at Justin and Heather in turn. "Did you two follow us after the Last Night concert?" she asked.

"I did," Justin admitted. "I wanted to hear what you were saying. I had to know if I was still a suspect. I hope you'll understand—"

Just then the phone rang. Justin picked it up, listened for a second, and handed it to Nancy. "It's for you," he said.

Nancy picked up the receiver. "Hello?" she

asked. "Oh, that's great! I'll tell everyone right now. Thanks so much for calling."

She was beaming when she hung up. "Fantastic news! That was Chief McGinnis. He just called the hospital, and Marcia's out of her coma. She's going to be all right!"

Everyone cheered.

"I guess everything worked out," Heather said pensively when the general rejoicing had died down. "Now that Brad and I are out of the program, Justin will get the job with Premier. And everyone will live happily ever after."

"Are you really quitting?" George asked, and suddenly Nancy remembered Heather's mysterious trip to Chicago.

"You bet." Heather grinned. "That's what Justin and I were arguing about that day in the mall. He really wanted me to stay in the program. He said I couldn't give it up. I told him I wouldn't stay in, no matter what he said. I even told the agency in person when I was in Chicago. The second the words were out of my mouth I knew I'd done the right thing."

The final pieces of the puzzle had fallen into place.

"Anyway," Heather continued, "now Justin's sure to get the job."

"Oh, I wouldn't be too sure of that," Nancy joked. "I've been thinking about signing up for the marketing program myself. I'd kind of like to give Justin a run for his money."

Ned pulled her close and kissed the top of her head. "You'd better not," he said tenderly. "Haven't you noticed? There's only one thing more dangerous than being a detective—being in marketing."

Nancy's next case:

A serious campus theft brings Nancy to Emerson College. Someone has stolen the critical compound CLT during a secret experiment at the biochemistry lab. All clues point to a group of student activists, but Nancy has other ideas.

The teen detective follows a twisted trail in her hunt for the mastermind behind the thefts. But before Nancy reaches the final turn, she finds a formula for the perfect crime—where the main ingredient is her own death . . . in *THE WRONG CHEMISTRY,* Case #42 in The Nancy Drew Files™.

Forthcoming Titles in the
Nancy Drew Files™ Series